A Deadly Lesson . . .

"I want you to hit the branch, but I want you to cut it in three. Start at the end, make three shots, and by the time you're done, the branch should be gone."

Mano studied the tree for a few moments, then turned to face it.

"No fast draw, Mano," Clint said. "Just show me what you can hit."

"Sí, señor."

He took a deep breath, drew his gun, then sighted down the barrel.

"Doing that, you're sure to miss," Clint said.

"B-But I must take aim."

"Don't aim," Clint said, "point."

Mano pointed his gun, but then dropped it.

"What you ask cannot be done."

Clint drew and fired three times rapidly. The branch grew smaller with each shot, and finally was gone. He quickly reloaded his gun before holstering it.

"Madre de Dios!" Mano said.

"Never holster your gun until you've replaced the spent shells," Clint said, "or someday you'll draw your gun and find the hammer falling on an empty chamber."

DON'T MISS THESE
ALL-ACTION WESTERN SERIES
FROM THE BERKLEY PUBLISHING GROUP

THE GUNSMITH by J. R. Roberts
Clint Adams was a legend among lawmen, outlaws, and
ladies. They called him . . . the Gunsmith.

LONGARM by Tabor Evans
The popular long-running series about Deputy U.S. Marshal
Custis Long—his life, his loves, his fight for justice.

SLOCUM by Jake Logan
Today's longest-running action Western. John Slocum
rides a deadly trail of hot blood and cold steel.

BUSHWHACKERS by B. J. Lanagan
An action-packed series by the creators of Longarm! The
rousing adventures of the most brutal gang of cutthroats
ever assembled—Quantrill's Raiders.

DIAMONDBACK by Guy Brewer
Dex Yancey is Diamondback, a Southern gentleman
turned con man when his brother cheats him out of the
family fortune. Ladies love him. Gamblers hate him. But
nobody pulls one over on Dex . . .

WILDGUN by Jack Hanson
The blazing adventures of mountain man Will Barlow—
from the creators of Longarm!

TEXAS TRACKER by Tom Calhoun
J.T. Law: the most relentless—and dangerous—manhunter
in all Texas. Where sheriffs and posses fail, he's the best
man to bring in the most vicious outlaws—for a price.

THE GUNSMITH

377

THE LEGEND OF EL DUQUE

J. R. ROBERTS

J

JOVE BOOKS, NEW YORK

THE BERKLEY PUBLISHING GROUP
Published by the Penguin Group
Penguin Group (USA) Inc.
375 Hudson Street, New York, New York 10014, USA

USA | Canada | UK | Ireland | Australia | New Zealand | India | South Africa | China

Penguin Books Ltd., Registered Offices: 80 Strand, London WC2R 0RL, England
For more information about the Penguin Group, visit penguin.com.

THE LEGEND OF EL DUQUE

A Jove Book / published by arrangement with the author

Jove Books are published by The Berkley Publishing Group.
JOVE® is a registered trademark of Penguin Group (USA) Inc.
The "J" design is a trademark of Penguin Group (USA) Inc.

For information, address: The Berkley Publishing Group,
a division of Penguin Group (USA) Inc.,
375 Hudson Street, New York, New York 10014.

ISBN: 978-0-515-15318-7

PUBLISHING HISTORY
Jove mass-market edition / May 2013

PRINTED IN THE UNITED STATES OF AMERICA

10 9 8 7 6 5 4 3 2 1

Cover illustration by Sergio Giovine.

ONE

WYOMING

Bill Werter stared down at his prize bull and shook his head.

"He lived like a king," he said. "It's a damn shame he had to die this way."

His daughter, Elizabeth, looked up at her father and asked, "But what will we do? We need a bull."

Werter looked at his twenty-year-old daughter and said, "Not only a bull, but a champion bull. We need a replacement for a king."

The vet stood up and faced Werter.

"You can't bring another bull here," he said, "or the same disease will kill it. You've got to wait until we get rid of it."

"How do we do that, Doc?" Werter asked.

The vet looked down at the dead bull, then back at Werter.

"We'll have to dip them."

"The whole herd?" Elizabeth asked.

Doc Tyler nodded. "Yep, all of 'em."

"That's okay," Werter said. "It'll take us time to find such a bull, and then get it here." He looked at Tyler. "Start dippin' 'em. I'll get Ed and the men to work for you."

"Okay, Bill."

Werter and his daughter left the barn.

Outside, Ed Hagen and some of the ranch hands were waiting.

"The king is dead," Werter said. "Ed, go inside. Doc Tyler will tell you what has to be done."

"Okay, boss."

"Take some of the boys," Werter said. "I'm going into town. I'll be back later today."

"Right."

Hagen took some of the men into the barn. Werter stopped one of the men and said, "Saddle my horse."

"Yes, sir."

"I'll come with you, Pa," Elizabeth said.

"No," Werter said. "Stay here. I'll be back later."

"What are you gonna do, Pa?"

"Send some telegrams," he said. "Find us a bull. Find us a new king."

It took several weeks, but in the end Bill Werter found his replacement. All that remained was to get the bull to Wyoming. It was a long way to come, and for that job he needed a special man, one he could trust with the money, one who could successfully make the trek.

"I'll go," Ed Hagen said.

"No," Werter said, "I need you here."

"One of the other men, then?" Hagen asked.

"Is there one I can trust to carry the money?" Werter asked. "And not be tempted to gamble it, or drink or whore it away?"

"No," Hagen said, "we have no men that trustworthy. Maybe not even me."

Werter looked across his desk at his loyal foreman and said, "I would trust you, Ed, but I need you here. And I'd go myself, but I'm too old to make the trip."

"You're only sixty, Pa," Elizabeth said from the door, where she'd been listening.

"And that is too old, my girl," Werter said. "What are you doing eavesdropping at the door?"

"It's the only way I can find out things," she said. "You won't confide in me, as you would a son."

"Forgive me," he said. "Come in and sit."

She nodded, entered the room, and sat alongside Ed Hagen, who loved her. At thirty-eight, though, he thought himself too old for her, and so he never spoke of it.

"I'm going to need the both of you in the weeks and months ahead," he said. "We've lost a lot of stock, and now our bull. But I've finally found us another one."

"Another king?" she asked.

"No," Werter said, "but a duke. El Duque, in fact."

"And where is El Duque?" Elizabeth asked.

"Mexico."

"Old Mexico?" Hagen asked.

Werter nodded.

"Mexico City."

"That's a hell of a long way," Hagen said.

"Well, outside of Mexico City, between there and a place called Queretaro."

"And how do we get it here?" Hagen asked.

"By wagon, mostly," Werter said, "some by rail. It's a long trip, there and back."

"And who could make such a trip?" Elizabeth asked. "And be trusted?"

Werter thought a moment, then said, "I know a man . . ."

TWO

Telegrams had become a big part of Clint Adams's life.

Maybe it was because he had a habit of responding to them. Whenever a friend sent him one asking for help, he got on his horse and rode. That's what it meant to have the Gunsmith as a friend. He was always there when you needed him.

On the other hand, he had received many telegrams offering him money if he would do a job. Unfortunately, most of those people wanted to hire his gun, and no matter how much money they offered, his gun was not for hire.

But when he rode into Fulbright, Wyoming, he was responding to a telegram that was both coming from a friend, and offering him money. He wouldn't know if he was going to accept the money until he knew what the job was. And he wouldn't know that until he got out to Bill Werter's spread.

But it was getting on toward dusk as he rode into Fulbright, and riding out to the ranch would have to be put off until the next day.

The telegram had reached him not in Labyrinth, Texas, where it had been sent to, but in a town called Tucumcari, New Mexico. His friend Rick Hartman had forwarded it to him there, and he had been riding the better part of ten days. It was time to give Eclipse some rest, even if it was only overnight.

He stopped at the livery, made arrangements to have Eclipse cared for, and then made ready early in the morning.

After that he got himself a room at the first hotel he saw. The type of room or price didn't matter; it was just for the one night. He dropped his rifle and saddlebags in the room, and then went for a meal. He found a small café, went inside, and ordered a steak.

He had signed his real name in the hotel register. He knew there was a chance his meal would be interrupted by the law. He was right. He was halfway through his steak when a man wearing a badge appeared at the door.

There were only a few diners in the place, as supper was over and most of the townspeople had gone home. Or they were in a saloon.

As the man approached, Clint studied him. In his forties, wearing a sheriff's badge, a worn gun in a matching holster. He'd been on the job for some time—maybe not this particular town, but he'd been behind some kind of badge for years.

"Mr. Adams?" the man asked.

"That's right."

"You mind if I sit?"

"I don't know," Clint said. "Am I in trouble, or can I keep eating while we talk?"

"No, no," the sheriff said, "you can keep eatin'. No trouble. I just wanna talk."

"Then have a seat, Sheriff," Clint said. "Can I offer you something?"

"No, thanks," the lawman said, sitting across from Clint, "I already ate supper."

"Coffee?"

The sheriff hesitated, then said, "Yeah, sure, coffee sounds good."

Clint waved to the waiter and pointed to his coffee cup, then held up two fingers. Sign language to waiters and waitresses was universal.

"Here ya go, Sheriff," the waiter said, putting a cup in front of him.

"Thanks, Nate."

Clint filled the cup from his pot, then went back to his steak.

"What can I do for you?" he asked.

"My name's Lane. I keep track of folks comin' into town," the sheriff said. "When I heard you checked into one of our hotels, I figured I'd just check in with you, see what your business is."

"How'd you know I was here?"

"Closest place to eat to your hotel. I figured you'd be needin' a meal."

"Good thinking," Clint said. "You been wearin' a badge a long time."

"This one for five years, but I been a lawman of one type or another for over twenty years."

"I figured."

"So, can you tell me what you're doin' here?"

"Sure," Clint said. "I'm passing through."

"On your way to where?"

"Bill Werter's place."

"The Big W?"

Clint nodded.

"You a friend of Bill's?"

"I am."

"Is this trip business or pleasure?"

"That's what Bill is going to tell me when I get out there," Clint said.

"You don't know?"

"Not yet. Bill just asked me to come and see him."

"Just like that, you came?"

"Just like that."

The sheriff sat back, sipped his coffee.

"Your friend's got hisself a lot of trouble out there."

"What kind of trouble?"

"Disease."

"His family?"

The sheriff shook his head.

"Cattle."

"Texas fever?"

"You'd have to talk to the doc about that," Sheriff Lane said, "and he's still out there, so you'll probably see him there."

"Okay, I'll ask him," Clint said. He finished his steak and pushed the plate away. "I'm going to get a beer to chase this down. You want to join me?"

"Sure," Sheriff Lane said. "Let's go over to the Brass Bucket."

"Big place?"

"The biggest."

"Take me to a small saloon, with only a few people."

"We got that, too," Lane said. "Let's go."

THREE

The sheriff took Clint to a small saloon that had a sign above the door that simply said SALOON. Inside they bellied up to the bar and ordered two beers from a sleepy-looking bartender named Ernie.

"What do you know about Bill Werter's family?" Lane asked Clint.

"The last time I saw him, he had a wife and a daughter. I think she was about fourteen."

"Well, she's about twenty now," the lawman said, "and his wife's been dead three years."

"I'm sorry to hear that. How did she die?"

"Fever."

"So he lost his wife to a fever, and now he's losing cattle?"

"He's had it rough."

"If I know Bill," Clint said, "he's making a go of it."

"He was, until this fever came along."

"Well," Clint said, "he'll beat this, too. Maybe he wants me to help him."

"What do you know about Texas fever?" Lane asked.

"I've seen it. That's about all."

"Then what could you do?"

"Like I told you," Clint said. "I won't know 'til I talk to him."

"Well," Lane said, raising his mug, "I hope you can find a way to help him."

"I hope I can," Clint said.

He only had one beer with the lawman, then left him at the saloon and went back to his room.

At the ranch several conversations were taking place. In Bill Werter's office, he sat with his daughter, Elizabeth.

"Pa, do you think Mr. Adams will really come?" she asked.

"His telegram said he was on his way. If he doesn't get here today, my money says he'll be here tomorrow."

"I hope so."

"Don't worry," Werter said, "Clint is a man of his word."

"I remember him being very handsome."

"Well, that's a young girl's memory," Werter said. "He's just a man, Lizzie."

"Well, I guess we'll see. Good night, Pa."

As Elizabeth left the office, she passed Ed Hagen, who stepped aside and said, "Good night, Miss Werter."

"Good night, Ed."

Werter chuckled as Hagen entered the room and sat down.

"Why don't you tell that gal how you feel, Ed?" he asked.

"Whataya mean, boss?"

"You think I can't see how you feel about her?"

"Aw, shucks, boss," Hagen said. "I'm plumb too old for Miss Elizabeth."

"Well, why don't you start by just calling her Elizabeth? Or Lizzie?"

"I couldn't do that."

"Well," Werter said, "maybe one day. What's on your mind?"

"Doc says we got most of the herd dipped," Hagen said. "He says if Adams comes back with that bull in a month or more, it should be okay."

"A month, huh? Might take longer than that."

"I got somethin' to tell you, boss."

"What's that?"

"The word's got out about El Duque, and you sending a man to pick him up."

"So?"

"The word's also out on how much money he'll be carryin'—thousands of dollars."

"Damn," Werter said. "That ain't going to make Clint's job any easier."

"No, it ain't," Hagen said.

"They'll try to kill him on the way to Mexico for the money, or on the way back for the bull."

"If he takes the job," Hagen added.

"Oh, don't worry," Werter said. "He'll do it. The only question is, will he do it as a favor or as a job?"

"You think he'll turn down the money?"

"I don't know," Werter said. "It's been five years since I've seen him."

"But you still think he's comin'?"

"Like I told Lizzie," Werter said, "he'll be here. That's what his telegram said."

"Okay, boss," Hagen said, "like you say." He stood up. "Night."

"Night, Ed."

The foreman left and Werter sat back in his chair, hoping he was right about his friend, even after five years.

Outside the bunkhouse two hands, Branch and Dunwoody, were talking with their heads close together.

Branch said, "That's a heckuva lot of money."

"Yeah, but Mr. Werter," Dunwoody said, "he's the boss."

"Yeah, he is."

"Well, you ain't thinkin' of tryin' to steal that money, are ya?"

"Hell, no," Branch lied. "Course I ain't thinkin' of that. I'm just sayin', is all."

"I got to get to bed, Branch," Dunwoody said.

"Yeah, go ahead," Branch said. "Night."

Branch had talked to four of the men now, and still hadn't found anyone to help him steal that money, but he knew there had to be other men in the crew who felt the way he did. Sooner or later, he'd find someone to help him take that money from whoever Werter trusted with it.

Sooner or later.

FOUR

Clint woke up the next morning, checked out of the hotel, and walked to the livery. The liveryman had Eclipse all ready for him.

"Thanks," Clint said.

"My pleasure havin' that animal in my barn, Mr. Adams," the man said.

Clint mounted up and rode out of town, heading for the Big W spread.

As Clint rode up to the main house, a few hands turned from what they were doing in the corral to watch. Another man came out of the barn at the sound of his approaching horse.

"Can I help you?"

"I'm looking for Bill Werter," Clint said.

"You Adams?"

"That's right." He dismounted.

"I'm Ed Hagen," the man said. "Foreman."

"Glad to meet you."

"The boss has been waitin' for you real anxious-like," Hagen said. "Come on, I'll have somebody take your horse to the barn and I'll take you inside."

"Okay."

The foreman waved a man over and handed him Eclipse's reins.

"Watch out for him," Clint said, "he'll take off your finger."

"Yessir," the hand said.

Hagen walked Clint into the house and down a hall to Werter's office.

"Boss," he said, "Mr. Adams is here."

Werter looked up from his desk, smiled, and jumped up. He rushed across the room with his hand out.

"Clint! It's great to see you."

"Bill," Clint said, pumping Werter's hand.

"You met my foreman, Ed."

"Yeah, we met."

"Well, sit down, sit down," Werter said. "I've been on the edge of my seat waiting for you."

The two men sat across the desk from each other.

"Boss, you want me to go?" Ed Hagen asked.

"No, Ed, stay," Werter said. "This concerns you, too."

Hagen moved over by a wall and leaned against it.

"Where's Lizzie?" Clint asked.

"Upstairs," Werter said. "She's been anxious to see you, but let's get our business done first. You're gonna stay to supper."

"Sure," Clint said, "that's fine. Business first, Bill. I hear you've had some problems with your cattle."

"Texas fever, but we've got that covered, Clint. The doc has taken care of it."

"What do you need me for, then?" Clint asked.

"My other problem," Werter said. "The fever took my prize bull."

"And?"

"I'm buying a new one."

"From where?"

"Mexico."

"From who?"

"Rancher down there, a rich one," Werter said, "and he's going to be richer after I pay him for El Duque."

"El Duque?"

"That's the bull."

"How much are you paying?"

"A lot. I need somebody I can trust with that much money, Clint. Somebody I can trust to go down there, buy the bull, and bring him back. That's why I need you."

"Why not send a bunch of your men? Then they could watch each other."

"I think this is a one-man job, Clint," Werter said. "You'll attract less attention."

"You think somebody'll try to rob whoever you send down there?"

Werter nodded.

"Either on the way there or on the way back," Werter said. "The word has gotten out."

Clint looked over at Ed Hagen.

"I offered," Hagen said. "In fact, I'm offerin' to go with you."

"We can talk about that," Werter said to both of them. "After we agree to terms."

"I could do this for you, Bill," Clint said. "I mean, as a favor."

"No," Werter said, "this is a job, Clint. I'm going to pay you well. All you have to do is accept."

"It'll be a long trip, Bill."

"I know it. But I need that bull."

"All right, then," Clint said.

"You'll do it?"

"Sure."

"How much do you want?"

"How much are you offering?"

Werter looked at Hagen.

"Ed, I think you can go now," he said. "Clint and I can finish up here."

"Sure, boss."

"Tell the cook to add one for supper, will you?"

"Yes, sir."

Hagen turned to leave.

"And close the door on your way out," Werter said. "Thanks."

The foreman nodded, stepped out, and closed the door.

FIVE

In town, Sheriff Lane sat in his office with three men named Tibbs, Jerome, and Steiger.

"I'm pretty sure Adams is here to go and pick up the bull," he said.

"But where?" Tibbs asked.

"I've heard Mexico, but I don't know what part. That means you'll have to hit him on the way down."

"If we follow him, he'll spot us," Jerome said.

"How do you know that?" Lane asked.

"He's the Gunsmith."

"Don't be scared of his reputation," Lane said. "This is a lot of cash we're talkin' about."

"How much?" Steiger asked.

"Don't know," Lane said, "but we're talkin' thousands."

"And you're trustin' us to go get it?" Steiger asked him.

"Sure, I'm trustin' you."

"Why?" Tibbs asked.

"Because if you cross me," Lane said, "I'll just send three other men to kill you. It's easier to give me my split."

"And what is your split?"

"Even," Lane said. "I'm not greedy. The four of us split it evenly."

"Thousands?" Jerome asked.

"Five," Lane said, "maybe more."

"How much is that each?" Tibbs asked.

"At least twelve hundred," Lane said.

"That's . . ." Tibbs said.

"One thousand two hundred and fifty dollars, to be exact," Steiger said. "That's the split if it's five thousand."

"And it may be more."

The three hired gunmen exchanged glances.

"Whataya say?" Lane asked.

"Why don't you chuck that badge away and come with us?" Steiger asked.

"No," Lane said, "it's not enough money for me to throw everything away. But it's enough for me to send you fellas."

"After we kill Adams for that money," Steiger asked, "you're still gonna wear that badge?"

"Sure I am," Lane said. "I earned this badge, and every other badge I ever wore. But when you hand me my split, I'll have earned that, too."

"When is he leavin'?" Tibbs asked.

"Probably in the mornin'," Lane said. "If I find out for sure before that, I'll let you know."

"Okay," Steiger said, "we'll be ready to leave in the mornin'. I'll figure out a way to trail him without him knowin' it."

"I knew I could count on you," Lane said.

Steiger stood and the other two followed him out. Sheriff Lane sat back in his chair, hoping he'd have more information before the night was out.

Outside, Tibbs asked, "Are we really gonna give Lane a cut?"

Steiger looked at him.

"Let's see how much money we're talkin' about," he said. "If it's enough to take the risk, then fuck him. Let him stay here with his badge."

He looked at Jerome, who nodded.

"Let's get a drink," Steiger said.

Clint became reacquainted with Elizabeth over supper. She had changed from a gangly fourteen-year-old to a lovely young lady of twenty.

"I'm so glad you're going to help us, Mr. Adams," she said, passing him a bowl of mashed potatoes.

"When you were fourteen, you called me Clint," he told her. "Can you still do that?"

"All right, Clint."

After agreeing on his price, Clint had spent the rest of the day looking over the spread with Werter. It had grown by ten times since he'd last been there.

He also met the vet, Doc Tyler, who explained that they had the Texas fever beat.

"Just not in time to save the bull."

Clint took some potatoes, and passed the bowl to the foreman, Hagen. Then he accepted the platter of sliced beef from Lizzie, took two slices, and passed them on. Gravy, next. This was shaping up to be the best meal he'd had in months.

Around the table were Werter, Lizzie, Clint, Ed Hagen, and Doc Tyler.

"What's this new bull like?" Tyler asked.

"A little younger than the king," Werter said. "He's got a big rep down in Mexico."

"Why are they letting him go?" Clint asked.

"Because it's a lot of money," Werter said, "and because they have another one."

"A second bull?"

Werter nodded.

"Even younger."

"What's his name?" Lizzie asked.

"That'll be for Clint to find out when he gets down there," Werter said, "if he wants to."

"That doesn't really matter, does it?" Clint asked.

"No," Werter said. "Only if you're curious."

"Who are you buying this bull from?"

"Don Pablo Sandoval," Werter said. "His name's a lot longer than that, but that's pretty much it."

"Is he very rich?" Lizzie asked.

"Very rich," Werter said.

"Richer than us?" she asked.

Werter laughed.

"A lot of people are richer than us, daughter," he told her.

"Well," Clint said, cutting into his meat, "not really that many."

SIX

After supper Clint went into the sitting room with Bill Werter and the doc. They had cigars and brandy.

"You're not really plannin' on makin' this trip alone, are you?" the doc asked Clint.

"Why not?" Clint asked. "Like Bill says, I'll make a smaller target that way."

"Not with that bull in tow," Tyler pointed out.

"I'll worry about that on the way back," Clint said. "Maybe, when the money's been paid, nobody will care about the bull."

"He's still gonna be a valuable animal," Tyler said. "Somebody could grab him and ransom him."

"And I'd pay," Werter said.

"Again?" Tyler asked.

"Again," Werter said. "I need that bull, no matter how much it costs."

Clint drew on the very good cigar and sipped the excellent brandy.

"You're staying the night, of course," Werter said.

"Yes," Clint said. "And I'll leave in the morning."

"I will send a telegram to Don Pablo and let him know you're coming."

"And the price has been agreed on?" Clint asked.

"Yes."

"And what am I riding into?"

"What do you mean?"

"I mean, what are the feelings on the other side about Don Pablo selling this bull?"

"I . . . don't know what the situation is down there. Are you thinking that someone on that end might try to stop you?"

"Why not?" Clint asked. "Why should the situation be any different there?"

"So somebody from Mexico might try to rob you before you get there."

"Could be."

"Maybe you shouldn't do this alone, then," Werter suggested.

"It's a little late for that."

"I can still send someone with you," Werter said. "Ed, for instance—"

"I'd need someone I know I can trust to watch my back, Bill," Clint said. "That means someone I would pick out myself. That's what I meant when I said it's a little late. I'll be leaving in the morning."

Werter frowned.

"Maybe I should pay you more."

"It's not about the money," Clint said. He stood up, set the glass down. "I'm going to turn in."

"We'll have a good breakfast before you leave," Werter said, also standing.

"Suits me."

"I'll show you to your room."

They walked to the stairs together and went up to the second floor. Werter took Clint to one of the guest rooms.

"My room is all the way at the end, if you need anything," the man said.

"I'll be fine."

"Clint," Werter said, putting his hand out, "whatever happens, I appreciate you coming."

Clint shook the man's hand and said, "I'm happy to help—and make some money at the same time."

"I know you're not doing this for the money," Werter said, "but I need this whole thing to be a business proposition."

"Understood. Good night, Bill."

"Night, Clint."

Clint went into his room and closed the door behind him.

SEVEN

Harve Steiger woke the next morning and glanced at the whore lying next to him. He'd paid three dollars for her to stay all night. Three dollars was a lot when you were used to nickel night at the whorehouse, but he was already feeling richer.

She wasn't young, and she wasn't beautiful, but she had the kind of body he liked to be in bed with, big and meaty and warm. On top of that, she was a talented whore, and she liked her work.

She was lying naked, almost on her belly but leaning slightly on her left buttock. The right one was staring up at him, big and round and smooth. He smiled and slapped her on that cheek hard enough to leave the red print of his hand.

"Hey!" she shouted, sitting straight up in bed and staring around. "What the hell?"

"Rise and shine," he said. "Time for you to put that talented mouth to work, woman."

"What time is it?" she asked, yawning. She stretched at the same time, his eyes going right to her heavy breasts as they rose and fell.

"It's early," he said, "and I have to leave soon. So come on, let's go."

He got to his knees on the bed and took his flaccid penis in his hand so he could shake it at her.

She stared at his dick, then at his face, then back at his dick.

"Really? Is that supposed to put me in the mood?"

"I don't have time to put you in the mood," he said. "Come on, you're a whore. A dollar puts you in the mood, and I gave you three."

"I think you worked off those three when you stuck your tallywacker in my butt, Steiger," she said. "That hurts, you know."

"Then why were you moanin' and groanin' like you loved it?" he demanded.

"Because," she answered, "you gave me three dollars!"

"Whore," he said, "if you don't suck this cock, I'm gonna give you somethin' else."

"You don't even remember my name!"

"Wrong," he said, "I never knew your name, and I don't care. Suck!"

She glared at him, then got down on her belly, took his dick in her hand, and took it in her mouth. The flaccid thing just sat there, then started to swell slightly. She tickled his balls with one hand, stroked him with the other, while she increased the pressure of her sucking.

"And if you bite me, bitch, I'll kill you," he told her.

She considered it briefly, wondering if she'd be able to get out of the room before he could grab her by the throat, or grab his gun.

Clint awoke, got out of bed, and walked to the window, which overlooked the front of the house. There were already hands working with stock in the corral, and several men were riding out to do their chores. Clint had often wondered what it would have been like to settle down on a ranch. The times that he'd been a guest—like now—had already seemed pleasant, but he'd also been around during trying times, and he didn't think he'd be comfortable for very long. There was just too much to be done, and too many people to keep track of.

He washed up and packed his saddlebags for his trip to Mexico, then went downstairs for breakfast.

EIGHT

True to his word, Werter made sure Clint had a full breakfast—steak and eggs and flapjacks, along with some fresh biscuits. Lizzie was there to eat with them, but it was just the three of them.

"Clint," Lizzie said, "aren't you the least bit afraid?"

"Of what?" he asked.

"Well, of what might happen," she said. "Have you been to Mexico before?"

"Many times," he said. "In fact, I have some friends there."

"Then maybe they can help you."

"Maybe they can," Clint said. "I'll have to check while I'm down there."

"I'll certainly worry less if I know you have help," she said.

"About me," Clint asked, "or the bull?"

"Oh, you . . ."

After Steiger blasted his load onto the whore's face, he kicked her out of the room and got himself dressed. He'd gotten his three dollars' worth, so he gave her time to wash up first.

"Do me a favor," she said.

"What?"

"Next time you have three dollars, spend them on somebody else."

"I'll spend it on a whore who don't talk so much," he told her.

Once he was dressed, he went downstairs, found the sheriff in the lobby.

"I was just comin' up to see you," Lane said.

"You got more information?"

"I do," Lane said. "Let's find the others. I think I know the route Adams will be takin' when he leaves here. With that information, you can get ahead of him."

"That'll keep us from havin' to trail him," Steiger said. "He'll never see it comin'."

"Come on," Lane said, "let's find the others so you fellas can get goin'."

"If I know them, they're at the whorehouse," Steiger said. "Yesterday was nickel night."

After breakfast, Clint went outside to the barn to saddle Eclipse. Werter came in as he was tightening his cinch, carrying some supplies.

"I remember the way you like to travel, so I put some supplies into a burlap sack."

"Thanks." Clint took the sack and hung it on his saddle horn.

"And here's the money." Werter handed Clint a leather wallet. Clint took a look inside, saw a sheaf of hundred-dollar bills.

"And here's some spendin' money for you," Werter said, handing him another roll of bills.

"Much obliged."

"You want part of your fee now?" Werter asked.

"This isn't part of it?" Clint asked, indicating the roll.

"No, I'm coverin' your expenses," Werter said.

"Well then, you can pay me when I get back and the job is finished," Clint said. "Once that bull is safely in your corral."

They walked out of the barn together. Some of the men by the corral stopped to watch. Clint didn't see Ed Hagen anywhere, hadn't seen the foreman since the day before. Also, Lizzie was missing.

He mounted up.

"Was that true what you told Lizzie about Mexico?" Werter asked. "You got friends there?"

"I do."

"You going to try to get one of them to help you?"

"Maybe."

"What route are you going to take?"

"I'm not sure yet."

"You sure are closemouthed about this."

"I don't want anyone to know what I'm doing, Bill," Clint said. "After all, word got around about you buying the bull, didn't it?"

"You think one of my men talked?"

"One, or more."

Werter rubbed his jaw.

"I find out who it was, I'll fire his ass, and then burn it."

"I wish you luck."

"Naw, I wish you good luck, Clint," Werter said. "Send me a telegram when you get there."

"I will," Clint said. "See you soon."

Werter threw Clint a salute before he rode off.

Tibbs walked all the horses out of the livery and handed Steiger the reins of his. All four men mounted up and looked down at Sheriff Lane.

"You want us to kill 'im, Sheriff?" Steiger asked.

"I want the money," Lane said. "I don't much care how you get it."

"Okay," Steiger said. He looked at his men. "Let's go."

Lane watched the three men ride out, heading south. He only hoped the information he'd gotten about Clint Adams's route was right. The quicker Steiger and his men got this done, the faster he'd be rich.

Clint headed south from the Werter ranch, but as soon as he was out of sight, he headed west. This route would probably add a day to his trip, but he'd talked openly the day before about heading straight south. That meant he had no intention of doing so.

Besides, there was a little something he had to take care of in a town called Sublette.

NINE

Sublette was a busy little town that had only one thing Clint was interested in—a telegraph office. From here he could send a telegram without anyone being the wiser.

He rode into town and found the office immediately. He had more than a few friends who lived down near the border, and over the border in Mexico. Men whom he would trust to watch his back. There was a border town with a telegraph office, where he could stop in before crossing. He handed his messages to the clerk, asking for replies to be sent there. Hopefully, by the time he got there, the answers would be waiting.

"Send those right off, please," Clint said.

"Yes, sir."

He watched the key operator send the messages,

then left and walked with his horse to the saloon across the street. One beer and then he'd be on his way.

Steiger, Tibbs, and Jerome rode south and had to go only a few miles before Steiger realized what had happened.

"What is it?" Jerome asked as Steiger halted their progress.

"He didn't go south," Steiger said.

"How do you know?"

"No tracks."

"That just means he didn't go directly south from the ranch," Tibbs said.

"We're gonna have to fan out, look for his trail," Steiger said.

"What other way could he have gone?" Jerome asked.

"Lots of ways," Steiger said. "If I was him, I woulda gone east or west first, then south."

"What do we do if we can't find his tracks?" Jerome asked.

"We'll worry about that when the time comes," Steiger said. "Right now fan out and look real hard. I wanna pick up his trail soon."

"Yeah, okay," Tibbs said.

"If you see anything," Steiger said, "fire two shots with your rifle."

"Right," Jerome said.

"Now scatter!"

*   *   *

Sheriff Lane went back to his office after Steiger and the others left town. He did some paperwork, then left the office and went to the Brass Bucket Saloon. He got himself a beer, took it to a table, and waited. Before long the man he was waiting for came in, got himself a beer, and joined him. There was nothing strange about two men having a beer together. It all appeared very casual.

"The boys get off okay?" the man asked.

"Early."

"That's good."

"They headed south," Lane said. "I hope you're right about that."

"That's what Adams was talkin' about doin' last night," the man said. "If he changes his plan, the boys will have to adjust."

"They might not be smart enough to do that."

"Steiger's plenty smart," the man said. "The other two just have to do what he says."

"Maybe you better tell me exactly where Adams is goin'," Lane said. "Just in case the boys send me a telegram askin' me that."

The man hesitated.

"Come on," Lane said, "you already went against Werter by givin' me information. Where's the harm in tellin' me everythin'?"

The man didn't speak, just sipped his beer.

"Don't tell me you're feelin' guilty."

Ed Hagen stared intently at Sheriff Lane.

"Yeah, I am feelin' guilty," he said, "but that don't matter. I gotta start thinkin' about my own future."

"And with that money," Lane said, "you'll have a future, won't ya?"

"Yeah," Hagen said, "yeah, I will."

"Look," Lane said, "I'll get us two more beers and then you can tell me where Adams is goin'. If the boys can't pick up his trail, they can ride on down to Ol' Mexico and get there ahead of him. Be there waitin' for him."

"Yeah," Hagen said, "yeah, okay."

"Atta boy," Lane said, standing and slapping Hagen on the back. "I'll be right back."

TEN

Clint had himself a beer without attracting any attention to himself, then went outside, mounted up, and rode out of Sublette. From there he headed due south. Heading for Colorado. He thought about stopping in Denver to see his friend Talbot Roper. Maybe he could get Roper to tag along and watch his back, but he'd already sent the man a telegram. If Roper was available, he'd meet Clint at that little border town, or send him a reply. He had also sent telegrams to Bat Masterson, Bass Reeves, and a couple of friends across the border in Mexico. They all had their own lives, but if they were available, they'd be there to help him.

It would be some time before he reached the Mexican border. Riding through Colorado and New

Mexico, he might even think of somebody else he could ask for help. There was a man named John Locke who lived just outside Las Vegas in New Mexico. He was certainly a possibility. Looking for help from someone in Arizona or Texas would just be going too far out of his way. Don Pablo Sandoval was expecting him to arrive at a certain time, and to be more than a few days off from that would not do. The man undoubtedly had other offers for his prized bull. Clint had to get there in time, and make the buy.

It took them a full day to find his trail. They had to double back to the Werter ranch, pick it up, and follow it precisely. It led them to Sublette, where Steiger sent Sheriff Lane a telegram.

Tibbs and Jerome were waiting in the saloon when Steiger entered with the reply.

"What's he say?" Tibbs asked.

"He leaves it up to us," Steiger said. "We can follow his trail and try to catch up, or head for Mexico in a straight line and possibly beat him there."

He didn't add that the words "you idiots" were in the telegram several times.

"So," Tibbs asked Steiger, "what do we do?"

"Instead of trying to catch him, I'd rather get ahead of him," Steiger said. "Let's ride for Mexico."

"Now?" Jerome asked.

"After a quick somethin' to eat," Steiger said.

"Good," Tibbs said. "I'm starved."

*   *   *

Clint bypassed Denver a few days later and camped
just outside Canyon City. In the morning he'd ride in
and replenish his meager supplies. He thought about
stopping in Trinidad later in the week before leaving
Colorado, but Bat Masterson was long gone from
there. He'd rather bypass that town and then stop in
Taos for more supplies. He was only carrying enough
for a few days at a time, but a packhorse simply
would have slowed him down too much.

He'd been sleeping lightly when he camped, feeling that it was better to expect trouble than not. He
managed to get some sleep, depending on Eclipse to
warn him if anyone got close to their camp. The horse
was better on watch than most men Clint had ridden
the trail with.

He awoke in the morning, made himself some
coffee, and had beef jerky for breakfast before dous-
ing the fire, saddling up, and hitting the trail again.
He didn't see anybody trailing behind him, but more
important than that, he didn't have that feeling
between his shoulder blades that he got when someone was on his trail. That could mean only one thing
to him. He'd managed to hide his route from them,
so they were heading straight to Mexico, trying to
get there ahead of him.

At least that would make the ride to the Mexican
border less of a concern.

ELEVEN

MEXICO
JUST OUTSIDE QUERETARO

Don Pablo Maria Cortero y Sandoval stepped out onto the portico, holding in his hand a glass of sherry. His *segundo,* Carlos Montero, came from the other direction and stopped in front of him.

"Well?" Don Pablo asked.

"The bull is fine, *jefe,*" Montero said.

"Both of them?"

"*Sí,* both are fine."

"Good," Don Pablo said, "we want to make sure we sell our American friend a healthy bull."

"*Sí, señor.*"

Don Pablo studied the man for several moments, then said, "Well, speak up, man. You have something on your mind."

"It is El Duque," Montero said. "I do not think we should be selling him."

"We are not selling him, Montero," Don Pablo said, "I am."

"*Sí, señor,*" Montero said, "I understand, but I do not think—"

"I do not pay you to think, Montero," Don Pablo said.

"*Sí, señor.*"

"Go, see to the bulls," Don Pablo said. "Treat them both like royalty."

"As you say, *jefe.*"

Montero, a man in his mid-thirties, turned and left. Behind Don Pablo his wife stepped out onto the portico.

"My husband," she said, "do you think you should treat Montero in such a way?"

"I treat my men as I see fit, my dear."

"Yes, of course."

Antonia de la Huerta y Sandoval was some thirty years younger than her husband. They had been married two years, and she knew he had married her just to have her on his arm. He loved no one the way he loved his daughter, Katerina, who was only a few years younger than Antonia.

"Would you like another drink, my husband?" she asked, taking his empty glass from him.

"Yes, I would," he said. "*Gracias.*"

As she turned to go back into the hacienda, Don Pablo said, "Where is Katerina?"

"Your beautiful daughter is out riding," Antonia said.

"By herself?"

"I believe so."

"I have told her over and over—"

"*Sí*, but she is headstrong, is she not?" Antonia asked.

"Indeed," Don Pablo said. "Indeed, she is."

"I will get your drink, and then I must go to town. I won't be long."

"As you wish," Don Pablo said, turning away again.

Antonia nodded, and entered the house.

Montero went to the barn and saddled his horse. He rode away from the hacienda out into the hills west of the rancho. There he found Katerina Sandoval waiting for him by her horse. He dismounted and ran to her. Taking her into his arm, they kissed.

"Have you talked to my father?" she asked.

"I have."

"About us?"

"No," he said, "not yet."

"About what, then?"

"About El Duque."

She dropped her arms and stepped away from him.

"That bull!"

"He is selling your future, Katerina," he said. "Our future."

"It is only a bull."

"El Duque is a prized bull," Montero said.

"There is the other."

"Unproven."

"My father values him enough to sell El Duque."

"For money."

"Is money so distasteful to you?"

"I want only what you have coming," Montero said.

"And I want to be your wife, Carlos," she said. "You must speak to my father."

"I will," he said, "I promise, but the time must be right."

"And when will that be?" she asked.

"Soon," he said. "Very soon."

That did not make her happy.

"I must get back," she said.

He helped her mount her horse.

"My love," he said, "I promise—"

"I am beginning to tire of your promises, Carlos," she said, and rode away.

An hour later, in a deserted shack located farther west, Carlos kissed the smooth flesh of Antonia's breasts, teased her nipples with his tongue while she cradled his head.

On the outside the shack still looked deserted, but inside they had created a small love nest where they could meet and be together.

She reached between them to grasp his hard shaft and pull him toward her. She spread her legs and he pushed the spongy head of his cock against the wet lips of her pussy until they parted and he slid inside.

He slid his hands beneath her to cup the smooth orbs of her ass and began to move in and out of her. Her breath came harshly in his ear as the intensity of his strokes increased.

"Oh, yes!" she cried, biting him on the shoulder.

"Damn it!" he yelled, and increased his stroke until he was fairly pummeling her . . .

"I've told you not to do that," Montero said later.

"What?"

"Bite me."

She chuckled, rolled onto her side. Her small, exquisite breasts barely moved.

"You're afraid your young paramour will see it?" she asked.

"I don't need any trouble with Katerina right now, Antonia," Montero said. "And neither one of us needs any trouble with your husband."

She grinned at him and said, "However you look at it, Carlos, we are all heading for some trouble."

"Well, not yet," he said, pulling on his trousers. "First we have to deal with this matter of the bull."

"Why are you so concerned with that bull?" she asked.

"Because the bull is the future."

"Whose?" she asked.

"Ours," he said, although what he was thinking was, *Mine*.

He put on his vest and strapped on his gun.

"Are you going to get dressed?" he asked her.

"Yes," she said, "after you leave. You know I don't mind being watched while I disrobe, but not when I dress."

"Where does he think you are?"

"In town."

"Why?"

She shrugged.

"He never cares."

"Well," he said, "I must get back before he looks for me."

"When is this gringo supposed to arrive?" she asked.

"At the end of the month."

"Then it will all be over by then," she said, "one way or another."

"*Sí,*" he said, before leaving, "one way or another."

TWELVE

Clint arrived at the Mexican border with two weeks left to go on his trip. He thought about crossing at El Paso, but instead had chosen the small U.S. border town of El Codo. *El Codo* meant "The Elbow," which was how the town was shaped.

El Codo was of little significance, really. Across the river from it was the larger and more populated Mexican town of Nogales, but El Codo had something Nogales did not—a telegraph.

He rode into town late in the afternoon, which meant he was probably going to have to either spend the night there, or cross the river into Mexico and spend the night in Nogales.

He looked for and found the small telegraph office, leaving Eclipse unattended while he went inside to see if he had any replies.

"Why, yes, sir," the clerk said, "I believe they're right here."

The clerk went through a pile of messages, and just when Clint almost came to the conclusion that the man had lost them, he came up with them.

"Here ya go," he said, handing them to Clint.

"Is this all of them?" Clint asked.

"Yessir," the clerk said, "ya got three."

"Thanks."

Clint went outside to read them. Bat Masterson apologized, but he had recently taken a bullet in his thigh and couldn't ride. However, if Clint could find no one else, he'd wrap the thigh up as tight as he could, hop on a buckboard, and make the trip.

Bass Reeves was still marshaling in Indian territory, and had to testify in court, but if Clint couldn't find anyone else, he'd risk the wrath of the Hanging Judge and come to his aide.

The third message was from south of the border. Clint's friend Sebastián de la Vega had recently been thrown from a horse and the feeling had not yet returned to his legs. But he was sending someone to meet Clint in Nogales. He assured Clint that, despite this person's youth, he was very capable of watching Clint's back, and guiding him through Mexico.

Clint's first choice would have been Bat Masterson, but he wasn't about to make his friend travel while injured. His second choice would have been Talbot Roper from Denver, but he had not heard back from him. Roper was the best private detective in the country, and he was probably away from Denver on a case. Next would have been Bass Reeves, but he couldn't ask Reeves to go against the Judge.

So he was prepared to at least meet the man that de la Vega was sending him. He felt bad that his friend was paralyzed from a fall, and hoped that the use of his legs would return.

He went back inside and sent his own replies back to all three telegrams. De la Vega's man was probably already in Nogales, so even if he wasn't willing to use him, he couldn't stop him. He had to at least meet the man.

When he came out, he decided to go ahead and cross the river to Nogales and spend the night there. It would also give him more time with de la Vega's man.

He rode out of El Codo, found a shallow place in the river, and crossed into Mexico. Within half a mile he came to Nogales. It was getting dark as he rode in, and Nogales was alive with light, music, and loud voices. Clint felt lucky to find the livery pen so he could leave Eclipse there to be cared for, then he carried his saddlebags and rifle to a small hotel across from a noisy saloon.

"One night," he told the young clerk.

"Sí, señor." He handed Clint the key.

Clint went to the first-floor room, which was in the back, and dropped off his saddlebags and rifle. He didn't know where he was going to meet de la

Vega's man, so he decided to just get himself a beer, and something to eat.

He went back to the clerk and asked him where the best food in town was.

"Across the street, *señor.*"

"That noisy cantina?"

"*Sí, señor.* They have the best beer, the best *señoritas*, and the best *enchiladas* and *frijoles.*"

"And what about trouble?"

"It is not allowed."

"Really?"

"*Sí, señor.* The owner, he is my cousin, and he does not allow trouble."

Now Clint had to decide if the clerk was sending him there because it had the best food, or because the clerk's cousin owned it.

"I'll tell you what," Clint said. "If I pay you, can you get some food brought to my room from there?"

"*Sí, señor,*" the clerk said. "I can do that. Just tell me what you want."

"A little bit of everything," Clint said, handing the clerk some money. "Is that enough?"

"More than enough, *señor.*"

"Well, you keep what's left."

"*Gracias, señor.*"

The young man was in his twenties, and the extra money would be a good tip for him.

As Clint started back to his room, the clerk shouted, "*Señor*, what to drink?"

"*Cerveza!*"

* * *

Clint was sitting in his room when, a half hour later, there was a knock on his door. When he opened it, the clerk was there with two black-haired Mexican women wearing off-the-shoulder blouses, holding plates of food. The clerk was carrying a bucket of beer.

"Come on in," Clint said.

They entered and put the plates down on the top of the chest of drawers. The clerk handed Clint the bucket, which had kept the beer cold. To top it off, he handed Clint a glass mug.

"These are my cousins, Lupita and Consuelo."

Lupita was young, probably not yet twenty, and pretty. Someday she would be as beautiful as Consuelo, who was in her thirties and possessed of a mature beauty that Mexican women grew into.

They had brought him plates of enchiladas, tacos, frijoles, tortillas, sliced peppers and tomatoes, and beer.

It was a feast.

"Lupita and Consuelo can stay while you eat, *señor*," the clerk said, "and give you anything you want."

"I think I've got all I need," I said. "What's your name?"

"Eduardo."

"Well, Eddie, the girls can come back for the plates in about half an hour."

"The *señor* is sure he does not want us to stay?" Consuelo asked. "Maybe one of us?"

"Right now," Clint said, "the *señor* is only interested in eating."

Consuelo spoke to Lupita in Spanish, and the younger woman seemed crushed by what she'd been told.

"Sí, señor," Eduardo said, "they will return. Please, enjoy the food."

"Thank you, Eduardo," Clint said, "and thanks to all your cousins."

THIRTEEN

The food was delicious, and Clint was so hungry he ate almost all of it. Same for the bucket of beer, which held probably four mugs. He drank two and stopped, not wanting to alter his perception at all, not while he was carrying Bill Werter's money. That was also the reason he preferred to stay away from the lively cantina. There'd be plenty of men there drinking and having a good time, and every chance for trouble.

There was a knock on the door about forty minutes later, and while he was expecting Eduardo or one of his cousins, he still went to answer it holding his gun. When he opened it, a young man with a smooth, unlined face smiled broadly at him.

"Clint Adams?" he asked.

"That's right."

"I am here!" the young man said, spreading his arms wide.

"I can see that," Clint said. "Who are you?"

"I am Manolito!"

Clint waited a moment, then said, "Sorry, I still don't know—"

"De la Vega," the boy said. "I am Manolito de la Vega!"

"Ah . . ." Clint said, still unsure how to react.

"Don Sebastián is my papa," Manolito said, "and he instructed me to come to Nogales and assist his good friend, Clint Adams." The boy slammed his fist against his chest. "I am here!"

"So you are," Clint said. "Come in."

"Gracias, señor."

Clint allowed the young man to enter then closed the door.

"Ah, a feast!" Manolito said, eyeing the remains of Clint's meal. "I am very hungry after my long ride."

"Well, help yourself," Clint said. "I'm finished."

"Gracias, señor," Manolito said. He grabbed an enchilada in his hands and took a huge bite. Studying the young man, Clint could see the resemblance between father and son. They were the same height and build, though Manolito was slender. Clint had not seen Don Sebastián in about six years, but the last time he had, the older man was still standing tall, ramrod straight, with just the hint of a belly.

"There's beer in that bucket," Clint said.

"Ah, *gracias*!"

"If you're old enough," Clint added. The boy looked all of seventeen or eighteen to him.

"*Señor*, I am twenty-two," Manolito said. "I am a man!"

"Yes, you are," Clint said, "a young man."

Manolito drank some beer and wiped it from his upper lip.

"But a man, nevertheless," he said. He was dressed like a vaquero, with silver conches down the legs of his pants and on his vest, and a bolero hat hanging behind him, tied around his neck. He also wore a gun in a holster festooned with silver, the pistol itself bearing an ivory grip.

"Can you use that gun?" Clint asked. "Or is it just for show?"

"I can use it, *señor*," the young man said. "Perhaps not as good as you, but my father would not have sent me if he did not think I could be of use."

"No, you're probably right about that," Clint said, sliding his gun back into the holster hanging on the bedpost.

"I can show you if you like," Manolito said with a mouthful of frijoles.

"Perhaps tomorrow," Clint said. "Not tonight. You'll be needing a room."

"I have money, *señor*," Manolito said. "I can get myself a room. I just wanted to let you know that I am here."

"Okay," Clint said. "The desk clerk and his cousins

brought me that food, so when they come for the plates, you can get yourself a room."

Manolito picked up the last enchilada and said, "I should be finished eating by then."

True to his word, Manolito was wiping his hands on a cloth napkin when there was a knock at the door.

This time it was the two cousins, Lupita and Consuelo. Eduardo wasn't with them. As they entered, Manolito snapped to attention.

"Good evening, ladies," he said, removing his hat and bowing. "I am Manolito."

Consuelo looked at Clint, but Lupita clearly found Manolito interesting.

"He's the son of a friend," Clint said. "And he needs a room. Could you get him a key?"

"Sí, señor," Consuelo said, but instead of going herself, she turned and said something quickly to Lupita in Spanish. Reluctantly, the younger woman left the room.

"Is that your sister?" Manolito asked Consuelo.

"No, señor, she is my cousin."

"Ah . . ."

"But I am very protective of her," Consuelo continued, "as if she were my little sister."

"I see."

When she saw the empty plates, she said to Clint, "You were very hungry, señor."

"My friend Manolito helped me finish," Clint said.

Manolito smiled at her.

"That was very nice of him."

"Yes, it was."

"I am a very nice man," Manolito said, grinning happily at Consuelo.

She nodded and walked to the chest of drawers, started stacking the plates. Before long, Lupita was back with a key, which she handed to Manolito. The hot looks they were giving each other were unmistakable. Apparently, the young man had inherited his father's appetite for women.

"*Siete,*" she said to him. "Room 7."

"Why don't you show me the way?" he suggested.

Lupita looked at Consuelo, who nodded and said something in Spanish.

The two young people left the room. Consuelo went to the door and closed it.

"What did you say to her?" he asked.

"I told her she would not be needed anymore tonight," she said, turning to face him. Before he knew it, her loose blouse was over her head and on the floor.

FOURTEEN

Consuelo was a meaty gal.

Her breasts were big and bottom heavy, with large, brown nipples. She slipped off her skirt, then turned to show him her ass as she leaned against the door.

"Consuelo," Clint said, "I don't pay—"

"I am not asking you to pay, *señor*," she said, cutting him off. "I am not asking you to love, or marry. I am only asking that you—how do you gringos say it . . . fock?"

"Yeah," Clint said, "yeah, that's how some gringos say it."

She wriggled her ass at him, got up on her toes, then bent over so he could see her shadowy butthole.

"The men here they are . . . *estúpido*. They get drunk, they grab, they pay a dollar, grunt, squirt, and sleep." She looked over her shoulder at him. "You would not sleep after."

"Probably not," he said, then thought, Not with that body in bed with me.

Only they didn't make it to bed right away. He dropped his pants, didn't bother removing his shirt or his boots. He went over to her, slid his raging cock up between her chubby thighs, found her wet and ready, and entered her. He "focked" her that way, against the door. Every time he thrust himself into her, she rotated her hips and pressed back against him. He held her by the hips, tried not to trip and fall over his pants, which were gathered at his ankle. She grunted and groaned, her hands pressed tightly against the door, which vibrated every time their flesh smacked together.

She spoke in Spanish, very low so that he was only aware that she was speaking, but had no idea what she was saying. It was almost like a prayer. Then he grunted and exploded inside her so violently that it hurt. He withdrew his cock, which was still hard and pulsating, and glistening wet with her juices.

She looked over her shoulder at him, smiling lasciviously, and said, "And now, *señor*, we go to bed?"

"What else would we do?" he asked.

Lupita showed Manolito to his room, using the key to open the door for him, then holding the key in her hand and staring up at him.

"This is your room, *señor*."

"*Sí,*" he said, "this is my room."

"And your key." She held it out.

"Why don't you come inside, *chiquita*, and show me the room."

She pushed the door open and said, "There it is, *señor*. Your room."

"With a big bed," he observed.

"*Sí,*" she said, "a beeg bed."

From down the hall they heard the door to Clint's room vibrating on its hinges. It sounded like someone was lunging into it from the other side.

"I think your cousin is going to be busy for a while," he said.

"*Sí.*"

He hooked his finger into the neck of her loose-fitting blouse, pulled it down until her little breasts popped free. Her dark brown nipples were already hard.

"Come inside, Lupita," he said, "I have something to show you."

"Something beeg?" she asked.

"*Sí,*" he said, "something very beeg."

Clint and Consuelo moved the proceedings to the bed. He sat down and she got on her knees in front of him first. She took off his boots, then his trousers. He slipped his shirt off, simply pulling it over his head without unbuttoning it. His dick was standing up from his crotch at full attention, so she leaned in and took it in her mouth. Moaning, she began to bob up and down on him, bracing herself with her hands on his thighs. He sat back, leaning on his hands, and let his head fall back. She took every inch of his cock into her hot mouth, and it felt as if the back of her throat closed around him. She was very, very good at this.

He sat that way for a little while, then suddenly she let him pop free. He opened his eyes just as she threw herself on top of him, pushing him down to the mattress on his back. She reached between his legs, held his cock, and then sat on it, taking it all the way inside her hot, steamy cunt.

"Oh, Jesus," he said as her heat closed around him.

"*Sí,*" she said into his ear, "*Jesus Cristo!*"

After that, the bed began to jump.

FIFTEEN

Consuelo collected all the empty plates, then turned to look at Clint, who sat on the bed, completely spent. First he'd been riding for days, and then Consuelo had ridden him long and put him up wet. He was still trying to catch his breath.

"I bring you breakfast in the morning, *señor*?" she asked.

"I think," he said, "I better come over to the cantina for breakfast, Consuelo." He wanted to get an early start, and was afraid that if he let her in his room in the morning, that wouldn't happen.

She looked disappointed and said, "*Sí, señor.* Will I see you then?"

As she went out the door, he almost called her back, but decided against it. He really needed to get a good night's sleep, and if he called her back, *that* sure as hell wouldn't happen.

"Good night, *señor*," she said as she went out the door.

"Yeah," he said as the door closed, "good night."

In the hall, Consuelo encountered Lupita, coming out of Manolito's room. The younger girl took some of the plates from her. They smiled at each other and went down the stairs.

In the morning, Clint dressed, packed, and walked down the hall to Room 7 with his saddlebags and rifle. He banged on the door with the rifle butt. Manolito opened the door and peered out blearily. He was wearing his shirt, open, and little else.

"I guess Lupita got you to your room last night all right, huh?" Clint asked.

"What? Oh, yeah, she sure did."

"Well, get yourself dressed and meet me in the lobby in five minutes."

"Five?"

Clint held up five fingers and said, *"Cinco."*

"I understand," Manolito said. "I will be there."

Clint went downstairs and found Eduardo behind the desk.

"I'm checking out," he said, "and so is Room 7."

"Sí, señor," Eduardo said. "I hope you enjoyed your stay."

Clint wondered if Eduardo knew how much he had really enjoyed his stay.

"Yes, it was fine. Thank you for the food last night. I'll be going to the cantina for breakfast before I leave."

"My cousins will be happy to see you, *señor*."

Clint was paying the bill when Manolito came stumbling down the stairs.

"Sorry," the young man said. "I am not awake yet."

"You'll wake up at breakfast," Clint said. "Come on. I paid for your room already."

"I told you I have money."

Clint waved away the young man's protest and said, "Come on."

They left the hotel and walked across the street to the cantina.

"Is this where Lupita works?" Manolito asked.

"Yes, with her many cousins apparently."

"Male cousins?"

"I'm sure there are some male cousins," Clint said, "maybe even brothers."

"I don't like brothers," Manolito said. "I have never gotten along with brothers."

"You have brothers?"

"No," Manolito said, "I have a sister, and I know what I would do to any man who touched her. That is why I do not like brothers."

"Well," Clint said, "let's just go inside, mind our manners, and have breakfast. After that we'll be riding out of town."

"Mind my manners," Manolito said. "I can do that."

SIXTEEN

Two plates of *huevos rancheros* later, Clint and Manolito were sitting drinking coffee.

"How old did you say you were?" Clint asked.

"Twenty-two."

"Jesus," Clint said, "if I remember right, your pa must be in his sixties."

"Seventies."

"Potent bastard, isn't he?"

"He was," Manolito said. "My mother is twenty years younger than he is."

"Is she still with him?"

"She is."

"And your sister? How old is she?"

"Eighteen."

"Tell me about your father's injury."

"We had a horse on our rancho," Manolito said, "A black devil he was. No one could ride him."

"Don't tell me . . ."

Manolito nodded.

"My father insisted that someone had to break the devil, so he mounted him and rode him. He almost had him, too, but in the end the devil threw him, and then stomped on him, low on his back."

"What's the doctor say?"

"He may walk again, he may not," Manolito said. "It does not matter. He is still *El Patrón.*"

"What the hell was he doing on that horse at his age?" Clint said.

"My father will not bend to age," Manolito said. "If he had been able to ride, he would have come here instead of me."

"I never should have sent him that telegram."

"But you did," Manolito said, "and now I am here."

"Yes, you are," Clint said.

Manolito took his gun out and laid it on the table.

"You think this is only a pretty gun? It is not. I can hit anything I want to hit with this gun."

"A man?"

"Eh?"

"Have you ever killed a man with it?"

"No . . . not yet," Manolito said.

"It's not an easy thing, killing a man," Clint said. "Not an easy thing to do, not an easy thing to forget."

"Do you remember the men you killed?"

"Every one of them," Clint said. "They're in bed with me every night." Clint reached out and pushed Manolito's gun closer to him. "Put it away."

The younger man picked it up and holstered it.

"In fact, I think maybe you should go home, Manolito," Clint said.

"No, I cannot," Manolito said. "My father told me to come and help you, and that is that I will do. And you must start calling me Mano."

"All right," Clint said, "and you call me Clint. All I'll need of you is your knowledge of Mexico."

"You have it!" Mano said, spreading his arms expansively.

"I'm not going to want to run into any patrols while I'm in Mexico."

"We will avoid them."

"I don't trust the so-called law in your country."

"Who does?" Mano asked. "I will show you the way, but where are we going? And what are we doing?"

Clint told him.

"A bull?"

"A prized bull. El Duque."

Mano's eyebrows went up.

"I have heard of this bull," he said. "He is a legend."

"Well, he's a legend on his way to the United States."

"And you are a legend," Mano said. "Two legends!"

"Let's get going." Clint stood up, threw some money down on the table.

Consuelo and Lupita did not follow them out, did not beg them to stay. The two cousins had gotten what they wanted the night before.

Outside Clint looked up and down the street.

"There's something you should know," he said.

"What?"

"They'll try to stop us."

"Who?"

"Men," Clint said. "On both sides of the border. They'll try to steal the money I'm carrying, or they'll try to take the bull."

"Then I must tell you something."

"What?"

"I can guide you there, and we can avoid patrols," Mano said, "but that will be much more difficult coming back with a bull."

"Well," Clint said, "I guess we'll have to take our chances."

SEVENTEEN

"I don't like it down here," Tibbs said.

"What's wrong with it?" Jerome asked. "The women are fine."

"It doesn't feel right down here," Tibbs said. "Hell, we're in another country."

"So?" Steiger asked.

"This ain't America," Tibbs said.

They were sitting their horses on a hill, overlooking the flat desolate Mexican landscape.

"So?"

"What do we do if we run into the law?"

"Nothin'," Steiger said. "Right now we ain't doin' nothin' illegal."

"We ain't expectin' him to just come ridin' up on us, are we?" Jerome asked.

"No," Steiger said. "We'll have to find him."

"What? Down here?" Tibbs asked.

"Down here."

"Do you even know where we are?" Jerome asked Steiger.

"Of course I do," Steiger lied.

They left Nogales, riding side by side.

"My father told me about you," Mano said. "I mean, over the years, he's talked about you."

"He has?"

"Is it all true?"

"Since I don't know what he told you, I can't answer that question."

Mano studied Clint for a few moments, then said, "I won't tell you."

"Why not?"

"I think maybe I will find out during this ride."

"You might at that." Clint looked behind him.

"Are we being followed?"

"No."

"And that bothers you?"

"Yes."

"Why?"

"The word went out that I was carrying a large sum of money," Clint said. "I can't believe that nobody is going to try to take it."

"Then if they're not following us, where are they?" Mano asked.

Clint pointed ahead of them.

"Out there maybe."

"In front of us?"

"Best way not to be spotted following someone is to be ahead of them."

Mano reined his horse in. Clint rode a few feet on before stopping and looking back.

"What is it?"

"It is very easy to get lost in Mexico," Mano said. "Especially if you are a gringo."

"So?"

"If they are out there," Mano said, pointing south, "we should go there"—he pointed west—"or there"—he pointed east. "Let them try to find us, then."

"Lead the way," Clint said. "You're the guide."

Mano turned them west.

"If the word is out that you have a lot of money," Mano said, "then there are probably men on this side of the border looking for you, too."

"You're probably right," Clint said. "And they won't be getting lost, will they?"

They rode until dusk, avoiding the few small towns they came within shouting distance of.

"Should we make a fire?" Mano asked.

Clint thought a moment, decided in favor of it—mostly because he wanted coffee. But also because a fire out here wouldn't necessarily belong to them. There had to be other people setting up camp.

Clint built a fire, prepared coffee and beans, then passed Mano a plate and a tin mug.

"Hijo de un cabron!" Mano swore, after sipping the coffee.

"What is it?"

"That part of my father's tales is right," Mano said. "Your trail coffee is strong."

"The way I like it."

Mano put the mug down between his feet, scooped some beans into his mouth with a wooden spoon.

"He also said you were a great trail cook," Mano said, "and if you ever wanted to hang up your gun, you could run a fine chuck wagon."

"Not with the trail drives drying up," Clint said.

"My father would hire you," Mano said. "We still drive cattle down here."

"No thanks," Clint said. "For as many men who like a cook's food, there are that many who don't. You can't please everyone."

"Well . . . I like these beans," Mano said, holding the plate out to Clint. "More, please."

EIGHTEEN

Carlos Montero pulled on his boots and looked over his shoulder at Angelina Sandoval, lying naked on the bed. Her skin was dappled with perspiration.

"Where does he want you to go?" she asked.

"You should know."

"He does not discuss his business with me," she said. "I am only his wife."

"Mexico City," he said. "To the bank there."

"Why you?"

"I am the only one he trusts to carry money," Montero said.

"That must make you very proud."

He stood up, grabbed his gun belt, and strapped it on.

"It did once. But he still treats me like just another vaquero."

She sat up, wrapped her arms around her knees.

"And you want to show him you are more, right?"

"That's right."

"Well, now is your chance," she said. "Instead of going to Mexico City, you can stop that money from coming here. And get it!"

"I am not a thief!"

"You would not keep the money for yourself," she said. "You would hand it over to my husband. That would prove your loyalty to him."

"And if he finds out we are sleeping together?" he asked. "Would that prove our loyalty to him?"

She smiled.

"Don't you worry about my loyalty," she said. "Just do as I tell you."

Montero turned to face her, and there was nothing amorous about his attitude.

"That is what your husband keeps telling me."

"Carlos," she said, reaching out to touch his arm, "I value you as a man, and as an ally. Does my husband do that?"

"No."

"And what I tell you to do," she said, "is for the both of us."

He thought a moment, then said, "All right. What would you have me do?"

"Listen carefully . . ."

* * *

They broke camp, having ridden together for three days. Mano kicked sand on the fire, then turned to go to his horse.

"Hold on," Clint said.

"What?"

"It's time for me to see how you handle that gun."

Mano looked down at the gun in his holster, then put his hand on it.

"Do you want me to draw?"

"Do you fancy yourself a fast draw, Mano?"

"I am pretty quick, I think."

"Let me see."

Happily, Mano dropped his hands to his side, then went for his gun. He had barely touched it when he found himself looking down the barrel of Clint's weapon.

"Wha—" He had not even seen Clint draw, it had been that fast.

"It's not always the fastest draw that keeps you alive, Mano," Clint said, holstering his gun. "Being accurate is more important than being fast."

"I think I am accurate," Mano said, but he did not sound as sure as he had a few moments ago.

Clint looked around, then said, "Okay. See that dead tree over there? The branch sticking out?"

"You want me to hit the tree?"

"I want you to hit the branch, but I want you to cut it in three. Start at the end, make three shots, and by the time you're done, the branch should be gone."

Mano studied the tree for a few moments, then turned to face it.

"No fast draw, Mano," Clint said. "Just show me what you can hit."

"*Sí, señor.*"

He took a deep breath, drew his gun, then sighted down the barrel.

"Doing that, you're sure to miss," Clint said.

"B-But I must take aim."

"Don't aim," Clint said, "point."

Mano pointed his gun, but then dropped it.

"What you ask cannot be done."

Clint drew and fired three times rapidly. The branch grew smaller with each shot, and finally was gone. He quickly reloaded his gun before holstering it.

"*Madre de Dios,*" Mano said.

"Never holster your gun until you've replaced the spent shells," Clint said, "or someday you'll draw your gun and find the hammer falling on an empty chamber."

"*Sí, señor.*"

"All right," Clint said, "just hit the trunk of the tree."

Mano nodded, then drew his gun and fired three shots, all hitting the tree dead center.

"Not bad."

Mano replaced the spent shells and holstered the weapon.

"But that's different from shooting at a man," Clint said.

"When the time comes," Mano said, "you will be able to count on me, *señor.*"

"I hope so, Mano," Clint said, "for both our sakes."

As Clint turned away Mano said, "Clint?"

"Yes?" Clint turned back.

Mano took a coin from his pocket and flipped it into the air. Clint drew without hesitation. He fired three times. The coin jumped in the air three times before hitting the ground.

"Jesucristo!" Mano said.

He hurried to the coin and picked it up. It had a chunk taken out by each bullet. He turned to see Clint walking away.

NINETEEN

Clint and Mano finally had to stop for some supplies, so Mano recommended the town of Merced.

"It is small, and has a trading post," he said. "And no sheriff."

"Why is that important?"

"Around here the law reports to the soldiers," he said. "And we do not want to encounter the soldiers, *es verdad*?"

"It's true."

"Then a town without law is better."

"For now," Clint said.

They rode into Merced, reined in their horses in front of the trading post.

"I'll go inside," Clint said. "You can keep an eye on the horses."

"But I can order," Mano said. "You cannot speak Spanish."

"I can point," Clint told him. "You watch the horses."

"*Sí, señor.*"

Clint went inside.

Across the street, three men watched Clint and Mano ride into Merced.

"Know them?" Armando Masilla asked his two companions.

"No," José Cruz said.

"I do not," José Reyes said.

Because both of his men were named José, Armando referred to them by their last names.

"A gringo will have money," he said.

"How do you know that?" Cruz asked.

"Because all gringos have money when they come to Mexico," Armando said. "It is why they come here, to hide, and to spend their money on whiskey and our women."

"*Sí,*" Reyes said, "our women."

"And the other man?" Cruz said.

"He is no one," Armando said. "A sidekick."

"Sidekick?" Reyes asked.

"*Compañero,*" Armando said.

"Ah."

"You take care of him," he told Cruz. "Reyes and I will take care of the gringo."

"When?" Cruz asked.

"Now," Armando said, "right now. When the gringo comes out."

"Bueno," Cruz said. "We can use the money."

"Sí," Armando said, taking his gun out and checking it, "we can use the money."

The two Josés also took their guns from their holsters and checked them.

Clint bought some coffee, beans, beef jerky, shells, and a couple of sticks of hard candy. He and the clerk had no trouble making the other understand. He paid with U.S. money, which the clerk did not mind at all.

He stepped outside, carrying the supplies in a burlap sack, except for the two sticks of candy. He handed one to Mano.

"Do you think I am a child?" Mano asked.

"No," Clint said, "I thought maybe you liked candy." He put the other stick in his mouth. "I do."

Mano thought about it, then said, *"Sí,* I do, too," and put his stick in his mouth. It was peppermint, his favorite.

"Let's mount up," Clint said.

"We might have some trouble," Mano said.

"What do you mean?"

"Across the street," the younger man said. "Three men, who have been very interested in me since we got here."

Clint looked.

"And now they seem to be interested in me as well," he said. "I see what you mean."

The three men wore sombreros and bandoliers across their chests.

"Bandits," Mano said.

"It would seem."

"And you are a gringo," Mano added. "To them, that means you have money."

"And I actually do have money."

"*Sí*, but they do not know how much," Mano said.

"So you're saying this is a coincidence," Clint said. "That they don't know who I am or what I'm carrying, it's just that I'm a gringo."

"*Sí*," Mano said, "that is what I am saying."

"Fine."

The two men sucked on their candy and waited. Finally, the three men pushed off from the building they had been leaning against, and started across the street.

"Take the man on your right," Clint said, "and do not fire unless I do."

"*Sí*," Mano said, "you are the boss."

TWENTY

Clint moved to his left, away from the horses, and Mano followed.

As the three men approached, Armando was in the center, with Reyes to his left and Cruz to his right.

"Amigo," Armando called out.

"Are you talking to me?" Clint asked.

"We give you a chance to ride out, gringo," Armando said. "Put your money on the ground first."

"And why would I do that?" Clint asked.

"So that you may ride out of town alive, *señor.*"

"Well," Clint said, "I'm not putting my money on the ground, and I expect to ride out of town alive anyway. What do you think, Mano?"

"That sounds like a good plan, *señor,*" Mano said.

"There you go," Clint said, "my friend approves of my plan."

"Your friend is very young, *señor*," Armando said. "Perhaps we should give him a chance to think over his answer, huh?"

"He's very young," Clint said, "but he doesn't need time to think. And I don't have time to play games with you or try to save your lives. So if you're going to do something, do it."

That seemed to surprise Armando for a moment, and disconcert his other two men. They were wondering why the gringo wasn't a little more afraid.

"If not," Clint said, "we will mount up and ride out and you can wait and rob the next gringo."

The three Mexican bandits didn't move, so Clint walked slowly to his horse and mounted up. While he watched the three men, Mano also mounted.

Clint started to back away with Eclipse, while Mano turned his horse to ride out of town. That was what Armando was waiting for. He was smarter than Clint thought.

Once Mano's attention was diverted, Armando went for his gun. His two compadres followed. Effectively, Armando had turned a three against two situation into a three against one.

Clint drew, pointed, and fanned his gun, exerting enough pressure downward to keep the barrel from jerking. The three Mexicans danced in the street for a moment, then fell. Clint quickly reloaded as Mano turned.

"What happened?"

"It's over," Clint said. "Keep riding."

He holstered his gun and followed Mano out of town.

A couple of miles out, Mano reined his horse in and turned to Clint.

"What happened?"

"They waited until your back was turned to draw."

"But I was ready," Mano said, "ready to—how do you say?—back your play."

"I know you were, Mano," Clint said.

Mano shook his head.

"I still need to prove myself to you."

"The time will come," Clint said. "As a gringo in Mexico, I'll attract more attention. You'll get your chance."

Mano stared at Clint for a few moments, then said, "I think perhaps all of the stories my father told me about you are true."

"Maybe," Clint said. "The next time I see him, I'll have to ask him what he told you."

"I can tell you that," Mano said as they gigged their horses. "After all, we need to talk about something."

"Mano—"

"There was the time you faced the James boys . . ."

TWENTY-ONE

"We're lost," Tibbs said, "ain't we?"

"No," Steiger lied.

"Well," Jerome said, "then we don't know where we are."

"Look," Steiger said, "we know where he's goin', so let's just go there."

"Mexico City?" Tibbs asked.

"Near Mexico City," Steiger said. "The Rancho Sandoval."

"If he's so famous," Tibbs said, "everybody should know where he lives. All we have to do is ask."

"We will," Steiger said, "when we get closer. All we got to do now is head south."

Tibbs looked at Jerome, who shook his head and shrugged.

"Look," Steiger said, "we're just adjustin' to the situation, that's all."

"Well," Tibbs said, "we better get this job done, is all."

"We will," Steiger said, turning his horse south. "Let's go."

Days passed without incident, which suited Clint. They were camped one night and he asked Mano, "How far to Queretaro?"

"A day or two," Mano said.

"Depending on?"

"On how fast we travel."

"I don't want to push the horses too hard," Clint said. "We can keep up the pace we've been traveling at."

For a few days, they'd been living on beans and coffee, and Mano was hankering for something more.

"Can we buy some bacon at the next town?" he asked hopefully.

"Yeah, sure," Clint said. "Bacon and beans would be a welcome change."

"You have not told me if any of my father's stories about you are true."

"And I won't," Clint said. "That's up to your father to tell you."

"*Bien,*" Mano said, "then tell me this."

"What?"

"The story about the time my father fought five

Juaristas and defeated them single-handedly without weapons. Is that true?"

Clint studied the younger man across the fire, then said, "Well, yes, that's true."

"Ha ha!" Mano cried out. "That old man! He told me it never happened."

"Well, I suppose your father may have become . . . modest in his old age."

"What about the women?"

"What about them?"

"All the women my father is supposed to have had," Mano said.

"How many is that?"

"Many," Mano said, "many, many over the years."

"Well," Clint said, "I think maybe that is something I'll leave to your father to answer."

"He does have a young wife," Mano said. "I suppose the women could have been attracted to his money."

"Just remember," Clint said, "your father didn't always have money."

"That is true."

"I'll take the first watch," Clint said, intentionally changing the subject.

But instead of going to bed, Mano wanted to hear more stories. Or ask about them.

"What about the time with the three nuns?" he asked.

"What?" Clint asked. "Who? Me or your father?"

*　*　*

Carlos Montero wasn't sure he was doing the right thing.

He had gone to Mexico City, as Don Pablo had wanted, but he had also collected some men to help him with the gringo when he arrived, as Antonia wanted him to do.

The gringo was projected to arrive any day. So Montero decided to take his men to Queretaro and intercept him.

Now he was sitting in a cantina, drinking beer, while his men were in back rooms with two of the cantina girls.

What if the gringo bypassed Queretaro? What if he went directly to the rancho? It was too bad he did not have the gringo's name.

But how many gringos would be riding through, carrying a large some of money and looking for Don Pablo Sandoval's rancho?

"*Señor,* you would like some company?" a cantina girl asked. She was young, busty, with a wide, beautiful mouth that promised many things.

But Montero had enough problems with women, since he was sleeping with the *patrón*'s daughter as well as his wife.

"No, thank you," he said, "but I will have another *cerveza.*"

TWENTY-TWO

Clint and Mano rode into Queretaro the next morning. Clint decided he needed a bath before he presented himself to Don Pablo to buy his bull. The man was a Spanish aristocrat, so manners and hygiene were probably as important to him as the money.

"A bath?" Mano asked.

"Wouldn't hurt you either," Clint said as they rode in.

"But it is not Saturday night."

"That's okay," Clint said, "nobody is going to hold it against you."

"Well," Mano said, "this is a fair-sized town. Must be plenty of pretty *señoritas* who would like a man who has just had a bath."

"There you go," Clint said. "We'll spend one night

in a hotel in a real bed, have a bath, and then tomorrow we'll move on to the Rancho Sandoval."

"That suits me," Mano said.

"You might even send your pa a telegram and tell him where we are and how we're doing," Clint said. "I'm sure he's worried about you."

"I will do so, *señor*," Mano said. "He will be happy to hear from both of us."

They rode up to a hotel and reined in. Clint dismounted and handed Mano his reins.

"I'll get us a room, and you take the horses to the livery. You better warn them to take special care of Eclipse. And watch he doesn't take off any fingers."

"I will."

"You mind sharing a room?"

"I do not mind," Mano said, "as long as we don't have to share a bed."

"Nope," Clint said, "sharing a bed is not something I'm hankering to do either."

They split up there, and Clint went into the hotel lobby carrying his saddlebags and rifle.

Carlos Montero was starting to think he'd been a fool to let Antonia talk him into this. How was he going to identify the gringo with the money without knowing his name or what he looked like? Don Pablo must know the man's name—why had he never mentioned it to Antonia?

Montero was drinking in a small cantina when the two men he'd brought with him came in.

"Carlos," Mendez said, "two men just rode in. One is a gringo."

"Where'd they go?"

"One went into a hotel, the other to the livery stable."

"We need to find out if this is the gringo with the money," Montero said, getting up. "We will go to the livery and ask the other man."

"He is pretty young," the other man, Ibanez, said. "He should talk if we pressure him."

"Well, we will pressure him, all right," Montero said. "We will pressure him."

The three of them left the cantina and walked toward the livery stable.

Clint checked them in and went upstairs to look at the room. It had two small beds, with mattresses that were barely better than sleeping on the ground.

He went to the window and looked out, saw three men leaving a cantina down the street. One of them pointed to the hotel, then pointed somewhere farther along. The three men exchanged some words, and then continued up the street.

Clint had a bad feeling, and left the room.

Montero, Mendez, and Ibanez came out of the cantina, and Ibanez pointed to the hotel.

"The gringo went in there," he said, "and the other man went that way." He pointed toward the livery.

"All right," Montero said, "let's go to the livery and see what we can find out."

At the livery, Mano spoke with the farrier about Clint's horse, Eclipse.

"Do not worry, *señor*," the older man said, "I would only take good care of such an animal."

"Just be careful of him," Mano said. "He likes fingers."

The man held up his left hand, which was already missing part of a finger, and said, "Do not worry, *señor*. I have been bitten before."

"I can see that."

The man took the reins of both horses and walked them farther into the barn.

TWENTY-THREE

Montero and his two men approached the livery, and then stopped.

"All right," Montero said, "you two go in and find out what you can."

"What are you going to do?"

"I will stay out here and watch," Montero said. "I do not want you to be interrupted."

Mendez and Ibanez exchanged a glance, then turned and walked toward the entrance to the barn.

Clint left the hotel, looked around, determined that he was not being watched. The three men may have had nothing to do with him, but he still had a bad feeling, and over the years had come to depend on his instinct.

The three men were up to no good.

* * *

Mano turned to leave the barn, but his path was suddenly blocked by two men.

"Excuse me, *compadres*," he said. "You are blocking my way."

"Just take it easy, *chico*," Ibanez said. "We have some questions to ask you."

"I do not know either of you," Mano said. "Why would I answer your questions?"

"It would be much better for you if you do," Mendez said.

"Do not force us to be unpleasant," Ibanez added.

Mano had his saddlebags over his left shoulder, and his rifle in his left hand. That left his gun hand free, and he let it hang down by his gun.

"I do not want to talk to you," he said. "Stand aside."

But neither man moved, and Mano knew he could not avoid trouble. What he didn't know was whether or not this had anything to do with Clint Adams.

"What question could you have for me?" he asked. "I do not know you."

"The gringo you rode in with," Ibanez said. "Who is he, and why is he here?"

Well, Mano thought, that answers that question.

Clint approached the livery and saw one man standing outside, two standing in the doorway. He assumed Mano was inside. That meant the man outside was a lookout.

He changed his direction, headed for the back of the stable.

Carlos Montero watched as Mendez and Ibanez stopped in the doorway of the livery. He turned and looked behind him, and caught just a glimpse of Clint Adams before he disappeared behind the stable. Montero decided to follow him and see what he did. It might also give him some idea of who the gringo was.

"Why do you want to know that?" Mano asked.

"We are looking for a gringo," one of them said, "and we want to know if your friend is the one we are looking for."

"Why are you looking for a gringo?"

"That is not important," the other said. "Just tell us who he is."

"If I tell you who he is," Mano said, "you might not like it."

"Why not?"

"Because he might turn out to be somebody you don't want to have anything to do with."

"Never mind that," Ibanez said. "Does he have the money on him?"

"Ah," Mano said, wondering when Clint would come looking for him, "this is about money."

"*Sí,*" Mendez said, "it is about money. A lot of money."

"Well, then you have the wrong people," Mano said. "We don't have any money. Now let me pass."

Both men dropped their hands to their guns and tensed.

"You will not pass until you tell us what we want to know," Mendez said.

"Who is the gringo?" Ibanez asked.

Mano remembered something Clint had told him one night around the fire. That he'd never killed a man without giving him a chance to walk away. That he always tried to convince him to live.

"All right," Mano said, "but you won't like this. His name is Clint Adams, and if you don't let me pass, you will both end up dead."

TWENTY-FOUR

Clint found a side door to the livery, opened it, and stepped in just as Mano was introducing him to the two men.

". . . both end up dead."

"What?" one of them asked.

"Clint Adams?" the other asked.

"Sí," Mano said, "now step aside."

Clint eyed the two men and made a snap judgment about them. He thought Mano could handle them, but he made himself ready, just in case. He moved farther into the stable, into a stall alongside a horse.

Montero saw Clint go in the side door, decided he could not follow that way. He went around to the back and entered the stable that way, listening intently.

"I won't tell you again, step aside," he heard someone say.

He moved into a position from where he could watch.

Mano decided that taking the initiative might be the way to go, since these two seemed slow to make up their minds.

Mano drew his gun.

The two men seemed startled, and if he expected them to step aside or run, he was disappointed. They went for their guns.

"Don't—" he said, but even as he did, he was firing. He pulled the trigger three times, and the two men fell to the ground.

"Madre de Dios!" he swore, looking around.

Clint saw Mano draw, and knew what was going to happen. He drew his gun, but Mano reacted quickly as the two strangers went for their guns. The young man fired, then quickly glanced around.

Clint stepped out and said, "It's okay, Mano."

Mano turned and stared at Clint with wide eyes. Clint stepped past him and checked the two men.

"Are they . . ." Mano asked.

"Yes, dead," Clint said. "Reload and holster your gun. The law should be here soon."

"What will we tell them?" Mano asked.

"The truth, that these two men tried to rob you and you killed them."

"Well," Mano said, holstering his gun, "that is sort of the truth."

"Yes, it is. Did they ask about the money I'm carrying?"

"Yes."

"And that's when you told them who I was?"

"*Sí,*" Mano said. "I thought it would scare them. I did not want to kill them."

Clint looked out the door, did not see the man who had been on lookout. The shots probably scared him away.

"What is it?" Mano asked.

"There was a third man," Clint said. "He probably ran off."

"So what do we do?" Mano asked.

"We'll wait," Clint said. "The sound of the shots should bring the law. It would in most towns."

Mano looked around the interior of the livery.

"Where's the owner?"

"He must have run off, too," Clint said.

Mano looked down at the two men.

"The first time's always the hardest, Mano," he told the young man.

"Actually," Mano said, "it was a lot easier than I thought, even though I am not Clint Adams."

Montero heard the name "Clint Adams," and knew he had to get out of that stable. He hadn't bargained for having to deal with the Gunsmith.

He had to get back to the rancho.

* * *

Clint turned and looked at the back of the stable.

"What is it?" Mano asked.

"I heard something."

They both walked to the back. Clint looked around, directed his attention to the dirt floor.

"Fresh tracks," he told Mano.

"Somebody was here?"

"Yes," Clint said. "Watching you, or us."

"Then he heard who you are," Mano said, "and he ran."

"Yes," Clint said, "yes, you're probably right."

"Just hold it right there, you two!" they heard someone say from behind them.

TWENTY-FIVE

The sheriff walked Clint and Mano to his office at gunpoint, their guns tucked into his belt. He already had men removing the dead bodies from the livery.

"Have a seat, *caballeros*," he told them as they entered his office, "and start talking. I do not like having men killed in my town."

Clint looked at Mano and nodded. The younger man started talking, explaining that they had just ridden into town, that Clint went to the hotel while Mano went to the stable with the horses, where two men tried to rob him.

"And you killed them."

"*Sí,*" Mano said, "I had no choice."

"And are you a *pistolero, señor*?"

"I am not," Mano said. "In fact, those were the first men I ever killed."

"And you?" the sheriff asked.

"I was inside the livery, in the back," Clint said. "I saw the whole thing."

"It happened the way he said?"

"Just the way he said," Clint said. "I heard them asking about money."

"Well . . ."

"Did you know those men, Sheriff?" Clint asked.

"No," the lawman said, "I never saw them before today."

"So they're not citizens," Clint said.

"No."

"And it's our word against . . . well, nobody's," Clint finished.

The lawman took a deep breath, then took their guns out of his belt, and set them on the desk.

"Take your weapons."

They picked them up and holstered them.

"When will you be leaving town?" he asked.

"Tomorrow morning," Clint said, "and no later."

"That suits me," he said. "Do not disappoint me."

Clint nodded and headed for the door. Mano followed him.

"Where are you headed, *señores*?" the sheriff asked.

Clint looked at him and said, "That's not part of the deal, Sheriff."

Clint and Mano walked back to the hotel, went into their room.

"Well," Clint said, "now they know who I am, and where we are."

"They know we are coming," Mano said. "Didn't they know that anyway?"

"Yeah, I suppose they did," Clint said. "Look, we've got to get something to eat, and then come right back here. No more trouble."

"I agree," Mano said, "no more trouble."

"All right, then," Clint said. "Let's go."

Montero was on his horse, heading back to Rancho Sandoval. He couldn't tell Don Pablo that the Gunsmith was coming, because he wasn't supposed to know that. He could tell Antonia, though. See what she would do with that information.

The Gunsmith was coming to Rancho Sandoval to buy El Duque.

One legend was coming to buy another. How could he stop that?

TWENTY-SIX

Clint and Mano came out of the hotel in the morning, and walked to the livery. The sheriff was waiting there.

"Seeing us off, Sheriff?" Clint asked.

"Just making sure, *señor*," the man said, "and I am only doing my job."

"Yes, you are," Clint said, "and very well, too." Clint was referring to his handling of the shooting incident.

They entered the barn, saddled their horses themselves, and walked them out.

"*Señor*," the sheriff said, "I hope on the way back, you will take another route."

"We will, Sheriff," Clint said. "I guarantee it."

"*Gracias, señor.*"

Clint touched the brim of his hat, and he and Mano rode away.

Sometime later, Mano complained, "You let him run us out of town."

"It's his town, not ours," Clint said. "He had to save face. It did us no harm to let him."

Mano thought about that, then said, "I guess you are right."

"You stand your ground or fight only when it benefits you, Mano, and never just to do it."

"I will remember."

Carlos Montero reached the rancho a full half a day before Clint and Mano would. He went right to the barn and unsaddled his horse. When he turned to leave, he saw Don Pablo standing there, watching him.

"I do not understand you, Carlos."

"Patrón?"

"I have given you everything," Sandoval said, "and in return, all I expect is loyalty."

"I am loyal, *patrón*."

"Are you back, and prepared to work?" Sandoval asked. "Or will you be running off again on some mysterious personal task?"

"No, *patrón*," Montero said. "I am ready to work."

"Then get to it," Sandoval said. "Do not make me think twice about giving you your high station."

"No, *patrón*," Montero said, "I will not."

Sandoval regarded him for a moment longer, then turned and walked away.

Montero breathed a sigh of relief, and wondered when he would get the opportunity to speak with Antonia Sandoval.

Steiger reined in his horse and stared down at the Rancho Sandoval. He finally knew where they were.

Jerome and Tibbs came up on either side of him and looked down.

"Wow," Tibbs said, "that's a big spread."

"Sure is," Jerome said.

"You think we beat Adams here?" Tibbs asked.

"I do," Steiger said, although he wasn't sure.

"Unless we can keep him from reachin' there," Tibbs said, "we ain't gonna get that money from him. We're gonna have to try to take the bull."

"How the hell we gonna get a bull back to Wyoming?" Jerome asked.

"We'll let Adams pack the bull up," Steiger said.

"But how we gonna get the bull from him without havin' to face him?"

"He'll be concerned with the bull," Steiger said. "We'll get the drop on him, either goin' in or comin' out."

"It is over that rise," Mano said, "about an hour ahead."

"All right," Clint said, "it's taken long enough. All we need is no more trouble for one hour."

As if on cue, they heard riders coming up on them from the east. They both turned and Mano stood in his stirrups to get a good look.

"*Rurales,*" he said.

"Of course," Clint said. "One more hour was too much to ask."

"We can run for it," Mano said.

"Run where?"

"To the ranchero," Mano said. "Don Pablo will handle the soldiers."

"I'm not going to let the man see me for the first time, leading a cadre of soldiers onto his spread."

"So what do we do?"

"We just wait right here," Clint said, "and you let me do the talking."

TWENTY-SEVEN

The *rurales* approached. There were a dozen of them, with one man at the vanguard wearing captain's bars. The uniforms were all soiled, indicating these men had been riding for some time—or they were all pigs.

The captain was a man in his thirties, with dark eyebrows and mustache, lots of dark hair sprouting from beneath his cap, and from his open collar. He had a long, nasty-looking cigar in his mouth. If it had been lit at one time, it was not now.

"Señores," he said, "I must ask you please to stand fast."

"We already are, Colonel," Clint said, deliberately promoting the man.

"It is captain," he said, "Captain Ortiz of President Diaz's *guardias rurales*. And you are?"

"My name is Clint Adams," Clint said. "I'm an American. This is Mano de la Vega."

"De la Vega?" the captain repeated, giving Mano an appraising look. "You are related to Don Sebastián de la Vega?"

"I have that honor," Mano said. "He is my father—and a friend of Diaz."

"Indeed," Captain Ortiz said. He looked at Clint. "And what brings you to our country, *señor*?"

Clint could see only one reason to lie. He didn't trust the *rurales*, so if he said he had come to buy a valuable bull, they would assume he had money on him. And they might "confiscate" it.

"I rode down here to visit an old friend," Clint decided to say.

"And who is that?"

"Don Pablo Sandoval."

The captain sat back in his saddle, keeping his back straight. Within a minute of each other, he had heard the names "Don Sebastián de la Vega" and "Don Pablo Sandoval." These were not men to be trifled with.

"And from where did you come?"

"Texas," Clint lied.

"That is a long way to come for a visit, *señor*," Ortiz said.

"Yes, it is," Clint said, "but Don Pablo is a very good friend."

"And how did the young Señor de la Vega come to be riding with you?"

"Señor Adams is also friends with my father, as we said," Mano replied. "My father has been injured, so when we heard Señor Adams was coming to Mexico, he sent me to see him. I decided to ride down here with him."

Ortiz eyed Clint suspiciously.

"Your reputation is well known down here, *señor*," Ortiz said. "I hope you are not here to add to it."

"Not only am I not intending to add to it," Clint said, "but I'm sure what you have heard has been greatly exaggerated."

"Interesting . . ." Ortiz said. He leaned over a bit to look at Clint's saddlebags, which were not bulging. Neither was the burlap sack hanging from his saddle, but that seemed to interest the captain. That was okay with Clint, though, as long as they didn't try to search him.

"What is in the sack?"

"Coffee, beans . . ." Clint said.

"Alas," Mano said, "no bacon."

"No," Clint said.

"May I see?" Ortiz asked, extending his hand.

Clint hesitated, then said, "Sure." He handed the bag over. Ortiz in turn handed it to his second in command, who opened it and rooted around in it.

"*Sí, mi Capitán,*" he said. "Coffee and beans, and some dried beef."

He handed the bag back to Clint directly, who hung it back on his saddle.

"Captain," Clint said, deciding to take the initiative, "perhaps you and your men would like to escort us to Don Pablo's rancho?"

"No, I do not think so," Ortiz said, since Don Pablo was not a particular friend of President Diaz. "You and your amigo may continue. Perhaps we will see you once again on your way back to Texas."

"Sure," Clint said, "maybe then I'll be carrying something you can confiscate."

"Ándale, señor," Captain Ortiz said, "before I change my mind."

"Sí, señor," Clint said. *"Vaya con Dios, Capitán."*

"And with you, Mr. Adams," Captain Ortiz said, "and with you."

"Come on, Mano."

Clint and Mano rode away, aware that the captain and his men were watching them. They finally topped the rise and went down the other side, and out of sight.

TWENTY-EIGHT

They came within sight of the rancho.

"Well," Clint said, "that's impressive."

The house was sprawling, mostly wood and white stucco, with a courtyard in the center. There was a huge barn with a corral on either side, and a bunkhouse that would be the main house on any other ranch.

"It is a nice little place," Mano said.

"Little?"

"You have not been to Rancho de la Vega in a long time," Mano said.

"I see."

Clint was sure Mano was seeing through jaded eyes.

"Let's go down and introduce ourselves," Clint said.

They had to ride down a hill and across an expanse of desolate ground. They were still about half an hour away.

They could have been hit on the way down, but they weren't.

Steiger knew he'd made a mistake.

"Let's go get 'em," Tibbs said.

"We can't."

"Why not?" Tibbs asked.

Jerome saw it, too, though.

"We're too close."

"To what?" Tibbs asked.

"To the ranch," Steiger said. "If we hit them now, the shots will attract attention."

"We can get the money and get out of here before anyone from the ranch reaches us," Tibbs said.

Steiger looked at Jerome, who shrugged.

"Your call."

"I don't think so," he said.

"Steiger," Tibbs said, "you made a mess out of this."

Steiger backhanded Tibbs without warning. The man flew from the saddle and hit the ground with a solid thunk.

"You're probably right," he said, "but don't say it again."

Sitting on the ground, his butt feeling bruised, Tibbs wiped the mouth with the back of his hand, came away with some blood.

"Understand?" Steiger asked.

"Yeah," Tibbs said, "yeah, I get it."

"You got somethin' to say?" Steiger asked Jerome.

"Like I said," Jerome replied, "your call."

Steiger looked at Tibbs again, who was still sitting on his butt.

"Get mounted," he said. "We'll find a place to hit them when they leave with the bull."

Tibbs got to his feet and struggled into the saddle. Steiger glared at him, and the man kept silent.

Clint and Mano rode through the entry arch to Rancho Sandoval. Men working in the corrals stopped to watch as they rode up to the house. When they reined their horses in, no one moved.

They looked around, but no one approached them.

"What is going on?" Mano asked.

"I don't know," Clint said. "Just sit tight. Let's wait for them to make the first move."

Antonia heard the horses approaching, and ran for the front door. Montero had managed to tell her that it was Clint Adams coming to the rancho to buy the bull. This excited her—which suited him, because it kept her from being angry with him. She was determined to be the first to meet him when he arrived, so she had Montero tell the men not to approach any gringo who rode in during the next week.

She reached the front entry of the house well before her husband, and flung the door open.

* * *

Clint was looking around. When the door swung open, it caught his attention. He turned and looked in time to see a beautiful woman come out of the house. It seemed as if she had been running, but when she got outside, she slowed to a walk.

Mano saw her and was transfixed. She was the most beautiful woman he had ever seen.

She walked up to them, glancing at Mano, but for the most part, her eyes were on Clint.

"Señorita Sandoval?" Clint asked.

She smiled and said, "Señora, actually. Don Pablo is my husband. May I help you gentlemen?"

"My name is Clint Adams," Clint said, "and I'm here to buy a bull."

Antonia had a couple of hands come over to take care of their horses, and showed Clint and Mano into the house.

"My husband, Don Pablo, is in the courtyard," she said. "Please follow me."

"Lead the way, *señora*," Clint said.

She showed them through the house, which was very open inside, with few walls. One room just seemed to flow into another.

The courtyard floor was made from slate, and Don Pablo Sandoval looked up as they started across.

"Antonia . . ."

"This is Clint Adams, Pablo," she said. "He is here to buy the bull."

"Clint Adams?" Don Pablo repeated, standing up. "You are the Gunsmith?"

"That's right."

"And you are here to buy El Duque?"

"Right again."

"And this young man?"

"Don Pablo," Mano said, "I am Mano de la Vega. My father, Don Sebastián de la Vega, sends his best."

"Don Sebastián," Sandoval said. "I have not seen my old friend in many years. You are welcome, Mano."

"Thank you, Don Pablo."

"Later you will meet my daughter," Don Pablo said. "You will both stay to supper, and also stay the night."

"Don Pablo," Clint said, "about the bull."

"You will see him soon," Don Pablo said, "but it will be dark in two hours. I think you should freshen up for supper, and see the bull in the morning."

"We'd like to get started back," Clint said.

"It will take a while to get El Duque ready to be transported, *señor*," Don Pablo said. "I think you will be here until the day after tomorrow. Why don't you try to relax?"

"That sounds good to me," Mano said.

"I can have two of the guest rooms made ready," Antonia said.

"Well," Clint said, "it seems like I'm outnumbered. Okay, we'll stay."

"Excellent," Don Pablo said. "Do either one of you play chess?"

"I've played," Clint said, "but I can't say I'm very good."

"So much the better, *señor*," Don Pablo said with a smile. "I like to win."

TWENTY-NINE

When Clint came down for supper, he was surprised
to find two beautiful women waiting for him. They
were different, though, different enough to indicate
that they were not mother and daughter. He'd sus-
pected as much when he saw how much younger
Señora Sandoval was than her husband. The young
señorita had black hair and eyes, while Antonia was
fair-haired, with blue eyes.

"Let me present my stepdaughter, Katerina,"
Antonia said. "This is Clint Adams."

"Señor Adams," the beautiful young woman said.

"Señorita Sandoval," Clint said.

"Please," she said, "call me Katerina."

At that moment Mano came down, and when his
eyes fell on the younger woman, Clint could see that
the young man was smitten.

"Katerina," Clint said, "this is Mano de la Vega. Mano, Don Pablo's daughter, Katerina."

"*Señorita,*" Mano said. "It is a pleasure."

"*Señor.*"

"Oh no," Antonia said, "you young people should call each other by your first names. Is that not right, Señor Adams?"

"It is, *señora,*" Clint said, "if you will call me Clint."

They were all trying to decide what to call each other when Don Pablo walked into the room.

"Cook says supper is ready."

"Please," Antonia said, "follow me."

Clint followed Antonia, but Mano followed Katerina. They ended up seated at a long wooden table, the five of them. The cook brought out a roast, all sliced on a plate, and extra plates of vegetables.

"Was your ride down eventful, *señor*?" Don Pablo asked Clint.

"Very much so," Clint said.

"We ran into some *rurales* just about an hour from here," Mano said.

"Captain Ortiz, no doubt," Sandoval said.

"You know him?" Clint asked.

"I knew him when he was a *bandito*," Sandoval said. "Now he is a captain in the *rurales*. Sometimes I despair for my own country, *señor.*"

"Tell us of your other adventures, Señor Adams," Katerina said.

Clint opened his mouth to answer, then caught Mano mooning over the young *señorita*.

"I think I'll let Mano do that, Katerina," Clint said. "Go ahead, Mano. Tell them some stories."

Mano looked at Clint, who nodded.

"Well," Mano said, "there were three men who tried to take the money Clint is carrying to buy the bull . . ."

After supper, Don Pablo invited Clint for cigars and brandy.

"What about Mano?" the older man asked.

"I think he'd rather stay at the table and talk to your daughter. That is, if you don't mind."

"No," Don Pablo said, "he comes from a good family. Come with me."

Don Pablo led Clint to another room. This one had four walls, and when the older man closed the door, they had privacy.

He poured brandy, and handed Clint a cigar.

"I suppose we should sit down and talk business," Don Pablo said.

Antonia left Katerina in the company of Mano, telling them she'd be back soon. The young people did not mind her leaving.

She went out the back and met Carlos Montero behind the bunkhouse. They had agreed to meet there on the night the buyer arrived.

"You were right," she told him. "He is the Gunsmith."

"I am lucky I was not killed," he told her.

"You will need more men."

"More men?" he asked. "For what reason? He is already here. He is buying the bull."

"You will need more men to take the bull from him."

"Take it from him?"

"Yes," she said, "when he leaves here."

"But . . . when?"

"He is leaving the day after tomorrow," Antonia said. "You have until then."

"But . . . I will have to pay them."

"I have money," Antonia said. "Don't worry."

"But . . . the Gunsmith?"

"He's just a man, Carlos," she said. "Just a man."

She turned and melted into the darkness.

THIRTY

Since the price had already been set, there wasn't much talking to be done.

"I have the money on me," Clint said as they sat, "but it wouldn't be smart of me to hand it over before I see the bull, would it?"

Don Pablo stared at him.

"Of course," Clint said, "after I've received the hospitality of your house, I suppose I should—"

"No, no," Don Pablo said, "you are quite right, sir. Finish your brandy and bring your cigar with you. I will take you to El Duque."

Clint drank down his brandy and stood up.

"We will go this way," Don Pablo said, and led Clint through a pair of French doors.

They went out into the night and walked to the barn. A man turned and looked at them with wide eyes as they entered, then relaxed when he saw that it was his boss.

"Don Pablo," he said, "good evening."

"Good evening, Ramon. This is Señor Clint Adams. He has come to buy El Duque."

"Ah," was all Ramon said. He was a small man, older then Don Pablo. Had probably worked for the man for many years.

"Señor Adams, this is Ramon. It is his job to see that El Duque is ready to be transported whenever you wish."

"Well," Clint said, "it seems we settled on the day after tomorrow."

"As you wish, *señor*," Ramon said. "El Duque will be ready."

"And now," Don Pablo said, "we will show him the bull."

"*Sí, patrón.*"

Ramon led them past some open stalls to one that actually had a door on it. There was a padlock, into which Ramon inserted a key. Then he swung the door open and said to Clint, "El Duque."

Clint stepped up and took a look. A bull with a white blaze of a face looked out at him and blinked.

"That's the finest-looking bull I've ever seen," Clint said.

"That is the point," Don Pablo said.

"And he's a big one," Clint said.

"We have a cart that will fit him," Ramon said. "And a team to pull him."

Clint looked at Don Pablo.

"Included in the price?" he asked.

"Of course."

"Can I look him over?" Clint asked.

Don Pablo waved him in.

Clint entered the stall, put his hand on the bull's hind quarters.

"Do you know much about bulls?" Don Pablo asked.

"Not much," Clint said. "I've worked with cattle. This one looks sound enough."

"He would have gored most men by now."

"Gored?"

"El Duque does not have a pleasant disposition," Ramon said.

"But he seems to like you, *señor,*" Don Pablo said.

Clint stared at the bull, who was standing calmly, and then eased himself out of the stall.

"You can close it now, Ramon," Clint said.

"Sí, señor."

He waited until Ramon locked the door, then said to Don Pablo, "What's he weigh? A ton or more?"

"More."

"Almost three thousand pounds," Ramon said.

"Jesus."

"We have a sturdy cart, and a strong team for you," Don Pablo said.

"Well, all right," Clint said. "I guess it's time to pay the bill."

"Over another glass of brandy," Don Pablo said. "Come."

Back in Don Pablo's study, Clint handed him the leather wallet with the money in it. Don Pablo counted the money out onto his desk, then drained his glass and refilled it. He opened his desk, took out some paper, and wrote Clint a receipt.

"And now," he said, "we can join the others for coffee and flan."

Clint hadn't had flan in a very long time. He would have preferred pie, but he was in Mexico, so he said, "That sounds great."

There was a safe in the corner. Don Pablo knelt before it, opened it, put the money in, and closed it again, spinning the dial.

"Very well, then," the older man said. "Back to the dining room."

"Lead the way, Don Pablo."

THIRTY-ONE

Clint came down for breakfast the next morning, found Mano already there talking with Katerina.

"Good morning, Señor Adams," Katerina said.

"Morning, Clint," Mano said.

Clint returned the greeting and approached the table.

"Coffee?" the girl asked.

"Please."

She poured it for him as he sat.

"I'll tell the cook to bring breakfast out," she said.

"What about your father?"

"He will be down soon," she said, "as will Antonia."

Clint noticed she didn't say the name of her step-mother with much pleasure.

As Katerina went into the kitchen, Mano said to Clint, "She does not like her stepmother very much."

"I got that feeling," Clint said.

"She thinks Antonia married her father just for his money."

"Maybe she did," Clint said. "That's got nothing to do with us buying this bull."

"Did you see the bull?"

"I did," Clint said. "He's an impressive animal."

"So you paid Don Pablo?"

"I did."

"When do we leave with El Duque?"

"Tomorrow morning."

Mano looked surprised.

"Tomorrow. I thought you would want to leave today."

"They have to get the bull ready," Clint said. "So you'll have one day to work your roughish charm on Katerina."

"She is beautiful," Mano said. "My father would love her."

The kitchen door opened before they could go any further. Both Katerina and the cook entered carrying plates and bowls. At that moment Don Pablo entered the dining room.

"Katerina!" he snapped. "How many times have I told you not to help Cook serve?"

"Father," Katerina said smoothly, "we have guests."

"I am sorry, *señores*," Don Pablo said, "but my daughter has a habit of performing menial tasks that are beneath her."

"What about when I am married, Father?" she asked. "Won't I be performing menial tasks then?"

"If your husband so wishes, my dear."

"If her husband wishes what?" Antonia asked, entering the room.

"My daughter is helping the cook serve breakfast," Don Pablo said.

"Oh, Katerina," Antonia said, "you know how that annoys your father."

"Yes," she said, "I do," and flounced back to the kitchen for more. Antonia put her hand on her husband's hand and said, "Leave her to me."

"Someone must straighten her out," Don Pablo said, "and yes, I will leave it to you."

The cook came back in with Katerina, and breakfast was served. Katerina poured coffee for all the men, and then took her seat.

"I propose a toast," Don Pablo said, lifting his coffee cup, "to El Duque, who tomorrow will leave for the United States."

"Oh, Father," Katerina said.

"The purchase is complete," Don Pablo said, "and Mr. Adams will be leaving with the bull tomorrow."

"May I have a chance to say good-bye?" Katerina asked.

"Of course," Don Pablo said. "You have until tomorrow morning." He looked at Clint. "My daughter has formed an attachment to the bull, and thinks he is her pet."

"He is," she said.

"I'm not sure I like being in the middle of a family affair," Clint said.

"You are not," Don Pablo said. "I assure you. The bull is yours."

"Not mine," Clint said. "I'm just the messenger."

"You will treat him properly during the trip, won't you?" Katerina asked.

"Of course we will," Mano said. "I will make sure of it."

"Yes," Clint said, pointing at Mano with his fork, "he will make sure of it."

Katerina touched Mano's arm and said, "I know you will. After breakfast I will tell you the best way to handle him. He is like a lamb."

"That's right," Clint told Mano, "a three-thousand-pound lamb."

THIRTY-TWO

"We can't miss him this time," Steiger said.

"How do you figure that?" Tibbs asked.

"We know where he is," Steiger said, "we know where he's leaving from, and he'll have a bull with him. He can't hide, and he can't outrun us."

"You mean somethin' might finally go right?" Jerome asked.

"I mean it better," Steiger said.

"It ain't been our fault, ya know," Tibbs said.

Jerome nodded.

"I ain't said it's been your fault," Steiger said. "I'm just sayin' this time things will be different."

They all stared down at the Rancho Sandoval.

"So we gonna stay camped out here and wait?" Tibbs complained. "Ain't even gonna go into town?"

"We ain't goin' no place," Steiger said.

"Mexico City's not that far—" Tibbs started.

"We're not leavin'!" Steiger said. "We're gonna stay right here until Clint Adams drives out with that bull."

"What if somebody else tries to steal it?" Jerome asked.

Steiger turned his head and looked at him.

"What?"

"I said, what if somebody else—"

"I heard what you said," Steiger said. "What I want to know is, why did you say it?"

"Well," Jerome said, "it just occurred to me we might not be the only ones after this animal. Or after Clint Adams."

"I don't care who else goes after him," Steiger said, "or the bull. We're the ones who are gonna take it. Tibbs?"

"Yeah?"

"Make a fire at the base of this rise and put on some coffee," Steiger sad. "Jerome, you stay on watch up here. Let me know if you see anythin'. Got it?"

"I got it, Steiger."

"Good."

Steiger turned his horse and rode down the other side of the rise, where they and their campfire would be invisible from the rancho. He didn't like Jerome's question. What if there was somebody else after the bull? Somebody from right there in Mexico? It was a valid question, but Steiger wasn't going to worry about it too much. After all, they were right there on the spot, and nobody else was.

* * *

Carlos Montero knew which vaqueros on the rancho could be trusted, and which could not. And he knew who could be bought and who could not.

Esteban Volquez was easily the biggest man on the ranch. He was strong and he was reliable, once you got his attention. The problem was, he was dumb as a rock. But he respected Montero, and the foreman knew he could use that to his advantage. And once he had Volquez in place, others would fall in. Like Cruz and the gringo hand, Montgomery. Those two were not happy working as ranch hands. They wanted something more, and with that bull, Montero would be able to promise it to them.

That would be three men. He needed one more, a fourth, a man who was good with a gun. Not from up close, not for a showdown in the street with Adams, but someone who could hit what he aimed at from a distance with a rifle.

He needed a crack shot, a man with no conscience, and he thought he knew where to find him. All he needed was the right amount of money from Antonia.

THIRTY-THREE

After breakfast Clint took Mano into the barn to show him the bull. They didn't need Ramon to open the door. Mano was able to look between the slats.

"Hijo de un cabron," the young man said. "He is a beast."

"That he is."

"We will be able to handle him?"

"We will," Clint said, "but I thought Katerina was going to show you how."

"She is," Mano said, "this afternoon."

"You'd better watch yourself around Don Pablo's daughter, Mano," Clint said. "The old gentleman has plans for her."

"She has her own plans, Clint."

"And do they include you now?" Clint asked. "You

two have just met. Tell me, son. You don't already think you're in love with her, do you?"

Mano didn't answer. Not right away.

"I have had lots of girls, Clint," he said finally. "And lots of women. Older women. Women of all sizes."

"But this one is different."

"You see it, too?"

"I see . . . something."

"She's wonderful," Mano said. "She has a mind of her own, very willful, very strong."

"I'm sure her father doesn't like that."

"He does not," Mano said. "He wants her to do as she is told."

"Isn't that what Mexican women are supposed to do?" Clint asked.

"All women are supposed to do that," Mano said, "but not Katerina."

"I see."

"Her stepmother is the same way," Mano said. "Perhaps you have noticed how beautiful she is."

"I have."

"Well, Katerina is a lot like her, that is why they do not get along."

"You gonna take her away from all this, Mano?"

"I don't know, Clint," Mano said. "She—we will talk about it."

"Talk about it, Mano," Clint said. "Talk about many things."

"We will." He took another look at the bull. "Magnificent."

"Yes, he is."

"Have you seen the other bull? The younger one?"

"No," Clint said, "there's no need. This is the one we want."

"Well," Mano said, "I'll talk to Katerina on how best to handle him."

"Among other things," Clint said.

"Yes," Mano said, heading for the door, "among other things."

THIRTY-FOUR

Mano was gone five minutes when Antonia appeared in the doorway.

"May I come in?" she asked.

"It's your barn," Clint said.

"Oh, no," she said, entering, "it's my husband's barn. Everything on this rancho is Don Pablo's. Didn't you know that?"

"I'm starting to see."

"There's a tack room in the back," she said. "Back there."

"Is that a fact?"

"Yes," she said. "Join me there."

"For what?"

"For a talk," she said. "Maybe more. We won't be interrupted."

Her golden hair glowed; her blue eyes were shining.

"All right."

She led him to the tack room in the back, closing the door behind them and locking it. The room was filled with all sorts of equipment, on the floor and hanging on the wall, but there was also a cot there, which made him wonder how much use the room got as something other than a place to store tack. There was no doubt what was going to happen now. Clint felt foolish to let it happen, but when he turned and looked at her again, he saw he had no choice. This kind of woman did not come along every day. She was beautiful, and willing, if not available.

The dress Antonia was wearing was a simple frock, probably chosen because it was very easy to get out of. She seemed to simply shrug, and it fell to the floor. Her body was breathtaking, full and smooth, pale and pink in the right places.

"Antonia," Clint said, "where is Don Pablo?"

"He is in his office, deeply involved in his paperwork," she said. "He stays there for hours."

The room began to fill with the scent of her, and his body reacted.

"And the ranch hands?"

"The vaqueros are out working," she said. "We will not be interrupted."

"Still," he said, "this is probably not a good idea."

She stepped out of her shoes, walked to him, close enough to put her hands on his chest, close enough for him to feel the heat coming off her body.

"Do you want me to leave?"

Hoarsely, he said, "No."

She rose on her tiptoes to kiss him, and he allowed his arms to encircle her. Her skin was as smooth as silk, and hot. He held her tightly as they kissed intensely. She kissed him the way a thirsty man drinks water when he comes in off the desert.

She moaned as they kissed, which only served to inflame him more. She struggled with his gun belt, so he stepped back from her to take it off and set it nearby. Next he unbuckled his trousers and dropped them, then sat on the cot while she removed his boots, and the trousers which had bunched around his ankles.

On her knees she undid the buttons of his shirt, slid her hands inside, and removed it that way, then leaned forward to kiss his bare chest. As she did, her hand encircled his hard cock, stroking it.

With both hands on his chest, she lowered her head and took his hard penis into her mouth. She moaned again as she sucked him, and he put his hand on the back of her head. She bobbed up and down on him, sucking him wetly. Then abruptly, she released him, climbed into his lap, and sat on his saliva-slick cock. As her heat closed around him, he groaned out load. She put her arms around his neck and began to rock on him. The wetness of her began to cover his inner thighs. She let her head drop back as she rocked, clasping her hands behind his neck. This gave him easy access to her breasts, which he ravaged with his mouth and teeth.

Abruptly she opened her eyes wide, stopped rocking, and pressed herself tightly down on him as waves of pleasure began to wash over her. She trembled, then suddenly began bouncing on him like he was a fucking bronco. In moments, he exploded into her, and it felt as if it was coming up from his ankles as he spurted his seed.

"Oh, God," she said, staring into his eyes, finally coming to a halt after milking him of every drop.

"You said it."

She kept her hands clasped behind his neck and pulled him forward into a long, steamy kiss.

"Oh yes," she said, a dreamy look on her face, "I knew it when I saw you."

"Knew what?"

"This," she said, wriggling her butt. He was still inside, and his cock was still mostly hard.

She was in no hurry to get off him, and he was certainly in no hurry for her to get off.

"Now we can talk," she said.

"About what?"

"El Duque."

"What about him?"

"I need him."

"For what?"

"To get away."

"Again," he said, "from what?"

"Not what," she said. "Who. My husband. Don Pablo."

"At the risk of repeating myself," he said, "why?"

"Because I made a mistake marrying him," she said. "He doesn't love me. He just wanted to be able to say he married me."

"So you didn't marry him for his money?"

"God, no," she said, "but I do need money to get away."

"So you want to sell the bull."

"Yes."

"But I already paid for it."

"I know."

"Wait a minute, Antonia," he said. "You don't want me to give you the bull, do you?"

"No. I want you to look the other way while I take it."

"I can't do that."

"Then I'll have to take it anyway."

"How do you intend to do that?"

"I'll have help."

"Oh, Antonia," he said, "that's not a good idea."

Finally, she slid off him and got to her feet. She started to get dressed, so he followed.

"So you thought by having sex with me, you could get me on your side?" he asked.

"Let us just say I hoped," she said, "but I'm glad

we did it anyway. I hope we will have a chance to do it again before you leave."

"I don't see how," Clint said, strapping on his gun.

She smiled, fixed her hair, and said, "I will find a way."

THIRTY-FIVE

Between Rancho Sandoval and Mexico City was a small settlement which had grown up around a mission. So it was called Mission, Mexico.

Carlos Montero rode into Mission and reined in his horse in front of the mission. As he dismounted, Padre Pete came out. He was a tall, dark-haired man in his forties, fully robed despite the heat.

"Carlos," the Padre said, "welcome. It's been a while since you attended mass."

"Padre Pete," Montero said, "is he here?"

"He's inside," Pete said.

"*Gracias.*"

As Montero started past the padre, the man grabbed his arm.

"No damage, please. The collection plate has been very bare these days."

"I am sure I can get the *señora* to be very generous, Padre," Montero said.

"Bless you, my son," Padre Pete said.

Montero went inside. Quentin was sitting in the first row, staring up at the massive crucifix behind the altar. Montero walked down the aisle and joined him. Even seated, the other man was a head taller.

"*Hola*, Quentin," Montero said.

Quentin looked at him, then back at the crucifix.

"Do you have my money?" the big man asked.

"I do."

Quentin put his hand out. Montero took out the money and handed it to him. The big man tucked it away in a pocket without counting it.

"When?"

"As soon as they leave the rancho," Montero said. "They will be moving slowly, driving the bull in a cart."

"Going in what direction?"

"South."

"How many?"

"Two men," Montero said, "but we will settle for just the gringo."

Quentin looked at him. He was thirty, looked forty-five, and had very intense, almost black eyes.

"I will decide that when the time comes," Quentin said.

"As you wish," Montero said.

"When?"

"Tomorrow."

"All right," Quentin said. "I will be there."

Montero didn't move.

"I must finish praying," Quentin said.

"Oh," Montero said, "*sí*, all right."

He stood up and walked back up the aisle. Padre Pete was still standing outside, looking off into the distance.

"Do you have a place for the bull?" Montero asked.

"I do," Pete said. "It will be safe."

"Somebody to care for it?"

"*Sí.*"

"It won't be for long," Montero said, "just until we can find a buyer."

Padre Pete shrugged.

"Will the Gunsmith be coming here?" he asked.

"No," Montero said, "he will be dead by the time we bring the bull here."

"You hope."

Carlos Montero hesitated, then said, "He *should* be dead."

"You hope."

"That is the plan."

"Plans do not always go according to plan."

Montero didn't like the sound of that.

"It must work," he said.

Padre Pete shrugged.

"I am sure if it does not, the *señora* will come up with another plan," he said.

Montero looked at Pete, opened his mouth to

retort, but they both knew that the plan was Antonia's, and not his. So if it didn't work, yes, she would have to come up with another one.

"I will see you tomorrow," Montero said, "with the bull."

"Will the *señora* be with you?" Pete asked.

"No," Montero said, "she will be staying away from this."

"Very smart," Pete said. "Smart and beautiful."

Montero walked to his horse and mounted up. The padre looked up at him. He had a serene, handsome, unlined face, and he smiled.

"Please tell the *señora* we miss her at mass."

"I will tell her."

The padre watched Montero ride away, sure that the foreman was Antonia's new lover. He knew the *señora* had left many lovers in her wake, for he was one of them.

Padre.

Lover.

Sinner.

And he'd still do anything she wanted.

THIRTY-SIX

Clint found Don Pablo Sandoval sitting in the courtyard, holding a glass. He immediately felt guilty for what had happened in the tack room, and swore to himself it wouldn't happen again. He didn't make a habit of bedding married women.

"Would you like some?" Don Pablo asked. "It is lemonade."

"Sure," Clint said. "Thank you."

Clint didn't know how, but the cook appeared with a glass for him a few minutes later, after he had seated himself across from Don Pablo.

"Thank you," he said, taking it from her.

"I need your help, *señor*," Don Pablo said.

"With what?"

"Your young man."

"Mano?"

Don Pablo nodded.

"I need him to stay away from my daughter."

"Well," Clint said, "we'll be leaving tomorrow. Is that not soon enough?"

"They are off together somewhere right now," the man said. "Do you know where?"

"No," Clint said, "but I'm sure they're not doing anything wrong. Perhaps they went for a ride."

"There are no horses missing."

"A walk, then."

Don Pablo put his glass down on the table near his elbow.

"I have plans for my daughter, *señor*."

"I imagine most fathers do," Clint said. "And I'll bet most daughters have plans of their own."

"She is my only child," Don Pablo said. "I am responsible for her."

"Isn't she an adult now?" Clint asked.

"She will always be my child," Don Pablo said.

"Well, I'm sure Mano is not trying to interfere with that."

"He might not be trying," he said, "but she is impressionable."

"Maybe she's been sheltered too long."

"Perhaps," Don Pablo said. "Perhaps I should show her more of the world, but she should see it with me."

"And not with Mano?" Clint asked. "Or any other young man?"

"Will you help me?"

"What do you want me to do?"

"When they come back," Don Pablo said, "talk to the young man. Tell him Katerina is very young."

"Mano is also young," Clint said.

"Young people are foolish," Don Pablo said, picking up his glass, "very foolish. And I don't know which is the more foolish, boys or girls."

Clint sipped his lemonade and wondered the same thing.

They had almost finished their lemonade when Antonia joined them, carrying a glass.

"What are you gentlemen talking about?" she asked.

"Business," Don Pablo said.

She looked at Clint.

"That's right."

"Business," she said. "Well, I know when I'm not wanted."

"Antonia," Don Pablo said, "have you seen Katerina?"

"She went for a walk with Mano," she said. "Don't worry, they'll be back in time for supper."

She turned and went back into the house. Clint noticed that Don Pablo did not look at her as she walked away. He put his glass down on the table, stood up.

"I think I'll go for a walk myself," Clint said. "Be back for supper."

"If you see Mano—"

"I'll talk to him, Don Pablo," Clint said. "I don't know if it will do any good, but I'll talk to him."

"Gracias."

"If you see Montero," Don Pablo said, "tell him I said he is to show you around the rancho."

"I appreciate that," Clint said. "It's an impressive spread. I'd like to get a look at it."

"Well, you can, if you can find Montero," Don Pablo said. "Of late he has been hard to locate. I am thinking about replacing him."

"Doesn't he do his job?"

"He does, when he is here."

"I'll have a look around," Clint said.

He went into the house, which was empty. He heard the cook puttering around in the kitchen, smelled supper cooking.

He went out the front door, looked around. There were several hands in the corral, but no sign of Carlos Montero. There was also no sign of Mano and Katerina. But Antonia came out the door behind him.

"Who are you looking for?" she asked. "Me?"

"No," he said. "Your husband is worried about his daughter. Did you really see her walking with Mano?"

"Yes," she said, "a few minutes ago."

"And what about Montero?"

He thought it was odd that she stiffened for a moment.

"What about him?"

"Have you seen him?" Clint asked. "Don Pablo

said he's been hard to find lately. He wants him to show me around."

"I don't know where Carlos is," she said, "but my husband is right. He has been hard to find lately."

"Your husband is talking about replacing him."

"I hadn't heard that," she said.

"Would it matter to you?"

"To me? No, I don't care. If you like, I can show you around."

"That would be okay," Clint said, "as long as we don't go to the tack room."

She smiled and said, "No, we'll leave that for another time."

Clint didn't bother saying he didn't think there'd be another time.

"Okay, sure, show me around," he said. "And maybe we'll find Mano and Katerina."

THIRTY-SEVEN

It was Antonia who showed Clint the new young bull.
He was kept in a covered stall out behind the barn.

"He's not as big as El Duque," Clint said.

"My husband says he will grow," Antonia said.

"Has he a name?" Clint asked.

"Not yet," she said. "After El Duque leaves, they
will move him into his stall, and give him a name."

"You don't agree with your husband selling El
Duque, do you?" he asked.

"No," she said, "I think he should have sold this
one and kept El Duque."

"Any sentiment in that opinion?" he asked.

She laughed and said, "No, I am not like Katerina.
I do not consider El Duque a pet. But he is proven,
and this one is not."

"What does Don Pablo say to that?"

"He says he can tell by looking at him," she said. "That he is a good judge of these animals."

"Well, he has the experience."

"For his sake, I hope he is right," she said.

They turned as they heard someone coming up behind them. It was Mano and Katerina. The young people were holding hands, but when they saw Clint and Antonia, they quickly dropped them.

"Well, hello, you two," Clint said.

"Hey, Clint."

"Señor Adams," Katerina said.

The two women did not greet each other.

"Is that the new bull?" Mano asked.

"That's him," Clint said.

"He does not look as big."

"He's not," Clint said. "But he will grow. This one probably weighs about twenty-two hundred pounds. El Duque is about three."

"I wonder why Don Pablo did not sell this one," Mano commented.

"Well, as I understand it," Clint said, "Don Pablo is a good judge of bulls."

"We had better get back to the house for supper," Katerina said.

"Why don't you ladies go ahead," Clint said. "Mano and I need to talk a little."

"About what?" Mano asked.

"Come along, Katerina," Antonia said, "we'll let them talk. Besides, your father has been looking for you."

"Is he angry?" she asked.

"Your father is always angry," Antonia said. "Isn't he?"

"I better go back and help Cook," Katerina said to Mano. "I will see you later."

Mano nodded, then turned to Clint.

"What's on your mind?"

"Her."

"Katerina?"

"Yes," Clint said. "Her father's got plans for her."

"She has her own plans, Clint."

"That may be," Clint said, "but we're leaving tomorrow, and she has to stay here and live with her father."

"What are you saying?"

"Just that there's something going on here that maybe you shouldn't get in the middle of," Clint said. "Something between a father and daughter."

"She wants to leave, Clint," Mano said. "She wants to see more than just this rancho."

"Well, she's not coming with us," Clint said.

"Then," Mano said, "I might not be going with you, Clint."

"That's up to you, Mano," Clint said, "but you will have to explain that to your father, and to her father."

Mano seemed to give that statement some deep thought.

"We better go and have supper," Clint said. "You can tell me in the morning what you've decided to do. I'll be leaving with the bull early."

Mano nodded, and they went inside.

* * *

The meal was a tense affair, with light conversation that masked what was really going on beneath the surface. The only one who wasn't feeling any of the tension was Clint. He knew what he would be doing the next day, and he knew what his intentions were.

After dinner he went out to the barn to talk with Ramon.

"Sí, señor," the man said, "I will have El Duque loaded onto the wagon, and the team hooked up. All will be ready for you."

"Ramon, has anyone been showing any interest in the bull lately?"

"Señor?"

"I mean any of the vaqueros, or perhaps even Montero?"

"No, *señor,"* Ramon said, "I have not seen any such activity."

"All right," Clint said. "I'll be out here early, even before breakfast." Clint intended only to have some coffee before he left. And he'd be able to carry more supplies than he had on the trip down, since he'd be driving the wagon with Eclipse tied to the rear.

"Very well, *señor,"* Ramon said.

THIRTY-EIGHT

Clint woke up in the middle of the night with a sudden thought. What if they were giving him the wrong bull? But El Duque would certainly be the older of the two, and he had seen both bulls. It was obvious which of them was the older. And while he wasn't an expert specifically on bulls, he could tell that El Duque was a magnificent animal. No, he was getting the right bull.

He settled back down on his mattress when he suddenly heard a sound from the hall. He realized then that it wasn't only the thought that had awoken him.

He eased his gun from the holster on the bedpost, left the bed, and moved to the door. Yes, he definitely heard someone moving in the hall. Maybe somebody wasn't waiting for him to get on the trail—they were going to make a try for him right now.

He waited for the right moment, and when he thought the person would be right in front of his door, he jerked it open.

"Oh!" Antonia said, her hand going to her chest. "You frightened me." She was wearing a frilly, filmy nightgown that left very little to the imagination. He was fairly sure she didn't usually creep around at night dressed like that.

"What are you doing?" he asked.

"Coming to see you," she said. "I told you I would find another way."

"Isn't your husband going to miss you?" he asked.

"We do not share the same bed, Clint," she said. "In fact, we don't even share the same room."

"That may be, but—"

"Do you really want to discuss this in the hall?" she asked. "Anyone could come along and see us."

As far as he was concerned, the only "anyone" who mattered at that moment was her husband—and perhaps her stepdaughter.

"Oh, all right," he said, "you better get in here."

With a big smile, she stepped inside.

"Are you going to shoot me?" she asked. "To keep me from ravishing your body?"

"Look," he said, walking to the bedpost and holstering the gun, "the tack room was one thing—and a mistake—but this is crazy. This is your husband's house."

"I know where we are, Clint," she said. "But you're leaving tomorrow, and this is our last chance."

"No."

"Really?" she asked, cupping her breasts through her gown. "You can say no to this?"

"I can, and I am."

She pulled the gown down to her waist, baring her lovely breasts. He licked his lips. She cupped them again, this time touching her nipples with her thumbs.

"Maybe," he said, "I *should* shoot you."

"Clint—"

"You better leave, Antonia."

She stared at him, then pulled her gown back up to cover herself.

"I could scream," she said.

"What would that accomplish?" he asked. "Unless you're hoping I'll kill your husband when he comes bursting in?"

"No," she said, "no, of course not."

She left his room, first checking the hall to be sure it was empty. He had to give her credit, she left with dignity, and with no sign of embarrassment.

He went to his door to make sure it was locked, but before he could do so, he heard a sound in the hall again. Was she coming back? Without retrieving his gun from his holster, he swung the door open again, catching Mano right in the midst of sneaking down the hall.

"Buenas tardes," Mano said.

"Mano," he said, "are you coming from or going to Katerina's room?"

"Uh . . . coming from."

"Well, get back to your room before someone sees you, and do it quietly."

"*Sí*, I will do so."

"I'll see you in the morning."

He closed the door, wondering if Mano had seen Antonia sneaking out of his room.

He went back to bed.

THIRTY-NINE

Clint came down the next morning and went right to the kitchen. The cook turned as he entered.

"Café?" she asked.

"Sí, por favor," he said, exhausting most of his Spanish.

She poured him a cup and handed it to him.

"Gracias."

He took the coffee out to the dining room, as Mano appeared.

"Are we having breakfast?" the young man asked.

"No," Clint said, "that is, if you're coming with me, we're not."

"I am coming," he said. "I told my father I would help you, and I will finish. Then I will come back here."

"Suit yourself," Clint said. "Get some coffee before we go."

"*Sí*," Mano said, then went into the kitchen and came out with a cup.

They were finishing their coffee when Don Pablo came down.

"Will you stay to breakfast, gentlemen?" he asked.

"I'm afraid not," Clint said. "We'd better get under way."

"Very well."

The three men went outside, where Ramon was waiting with a wagon—a cart, really—and a team. Inside the cart—fully enclosed within—was El Duque.

"There are supplies beneath the seat," Ramon told Clint. "Your horse is tied to the back. He almost bit my hand off."

"Didn't get a finger, did he?" Clint asked.

"No, *señor*," Ramon said, "I was too swift."

"Good." Clint turned to Don Pablo and stuck his hand out. The older man took it. "Thank you for your hospitality."

"And thank you, *señor*, for your . . . cooperation."

Clint wasn't sure what Don Pablo meant, but then the man looked over at Mano and he knew. Don Pablo thought Clint had talked Mano into leaving his daughter alone.

"You're welcome, Don Pablo."

"And I wish your employer luck with El Duque."

"I'll pass it on to him."

Clint climbed up on the wagon, picked up the reins. Mano walked behind and mounted his horse. Together they left the rancho.

* * *

"Steiger!" Tibbs yelled.

Steiger looked up from his coffee at Tibbs, who was at the top of the rise. Tibbs pointed. Steiger dumped his coffee in the fire and ran up the rise to join Tibbs.

"They just left," Tibbs said.

"All right," Steiger said. "Keep an eye on them. Jerome and I will saddle the horses. Make sure they go north."

"Yeah, okay."

"We'll give them a few miles," Steiger said, "and then we'll hit them quick, before they know what's happening."

Tibbs nodded, and Steiger went back down the rise to wake Jerome.

Behind the Sandoval house, Antonia met with Carlos Montero.

"Do you have your men ready?" she asked.

"I do," Montero said.

"And a place for the bull?"

"*Sí.*"

"Okay then," she said, "let them get a few miles away, and then take the bull."

"*Sí*, Antonia."

"And then let me know where it is," she said. "I'll come."

"We will take it to the mission."

"The mission?"

"There is room there."

"All right, then," she said. "The mission."

He turned to walk away, then looked back.

"Do you want them killed?"

She hesitated, then said, "Just take the bull, Carlos. However you can."

"*Sí*, Antonia."

She watched him walk away, then hurried into the house.

Katerina came out from hiding, not believing what she had heard. Her stepmother and her father's *segundo*, plotting to steal the bull from Clint and Mano. Should she tell her father? Would he believe her? Or should she warn Mano and Clint Adams?

She hurried to the barn.

FORTY

Clint reined the team in. They were good, strong horses, could pull the cart all day if need be. But there was no way they could ever run, not while pulling a three-thousand-pound bull.

Mano rode up alongside and asked, "What is it?"

"We're being followed."

"By who?"

"Three men," Clint said. "They were watching when we left. Don't look around!"

Mano had started to look, but stopped when Clint snapped.

"What do they want? The bull?"

"No doubt."

"So what do we do? Wait for them?"

"Well," Clint said, "there's no way to outrun them."

"When will they come?"

"I don't know," Clint said, "but we'll be ready, Mano. We'll be ready."

Mano leaned over and took a look into the back of the cart.

"El Duque looks okay," he said.

"We haven't even gotten started yet," Clint said.

Clint looked ahead. The terrain rolled. He wished it were flat, but they'd have to make do, be ready for somebody to pop up out of nowhere.

"Be ready, Mano," he said. "Don't wait for me to shoot."

"Yes, sir."

Clint shook the reins at the team and they got started again.

"We'll get ahead of 'em," Steiger said. "Find some cover to spring up from."

"Then what?" Tibbs asked.

"Then start shootin'," Steiger said. "Don't stop until the Gunsmith is lying on the ground, dead."

"Okay," Jerome said.

"But remember," Steiger said, "don't hit the bull. You hit the bull, then we got nothin'."

"We could go back, get the money that he paid," Tibbs said.

"You wanna ride into that ranch, with all them hands there?" Steiger asked. "Be my guest. Me, I'm gonna get my money for this bull."

"And then split it with Sheriff Lane?" Jerome asked.

"Naw," Steiger said, "he ain't been out here with us, ridin' around in this dust all this time. And he ain't gonna face the Gunsmith's gun. Naw, we ain't gonna split it with the lawman." In fact, Steiger thought, he wasn't going to split it with anyone.

They could see the wagon up ahead, but they were going to circle around and wait for them. Wait for them in a likely spot. The only way to be sure the Gunsmith was dead was to ambush him.

Men like that—like Adams, and Hickok, and Jesse James—you had to shoot in the back.

Carlos Montero sat his horse, looking ahead at the wagon, and the three men following it.

"Who are they?" Quentin asked. He had his reins in one hand, his rifle in the other. A big man, his big hands were no use for firing a pistol, but he was a dead shot with a rifle.

"I do not know," Montero said. "But we better watch them carefully. They might do our job for us."

"If I don't use my rifle," Quentin said, "I still get paid, right?"

"Oh, yes," Montero said, "you will be paid." He turned in his saddle, looked at Montgomery and Volquez. "We will watch awhile," he said.

They both shrugged. They didn't care as long as they got paid, too.

FORTY-ONE

The ambush came as expected, which, of course, meant it wasn't much of an ambush. But Steiger had messed this up from the beginning, with Jerome and Tibbs going along.

They sprang up from both sides, two from an old dried creek bed on Clint's side, one from a depression on Mano's side.

Mano took what Clint said about not waiting for him to fire to heart. His gun was in his hand before he knew it, but he rushed his first shot and missed.

Jerome was on Mano's side, and he rushed the young man and pulled him from his saddle before Mano could fire again.

Providence interceded on Clint's side. As Steiger and Tibbs rushed him, he drew and fired. His first shot hit Tibbs in the chest. But just as he fired his second shot, the cart's right wheel struck a rock. It jerked him just enough for his second shot to miss, and then Steiger was on him, pulling him from his seat . . .

"There," Montero said. "They have made their move. Quentin, get ready."

"Who?"

"Adams," Montero said. "Take the shot when you can."

Quentin shouldered the rifle.

Mano hit the ground hard, the air rushing from his lungs. Despite the fact he couldn't breathe, though, he knew he had to move. He scrambled away from Jerome, realizing that, somehow, he'd held on to his gun.

Jerome hadn't drawn his gun yet, but did so as Mano crawled away from him. The two men fired at the same time . . .

Clint also hit the ground hard, but managed to take the brunt of the fall on his left shoulder. He also held on to his gun, though with him it was no accident. He knew he was going to hit the ground hard, and he made sure he gripped his gun tightly.

Steiger had his gun in one hand when he grabbed Clint with the other. He meant to fire, but in pulling Clint from the cart, he lost his footing, slipped down to one knee. He put his left hand out to catch himself, while holding on to his gun with his right.

Both men ended up looking right at each other, each holding their guns, but pointed away.

The moment froze.

"You don't want to do this," Clint told him.

"At this point," Steiger said, "I got no other choice."

They both brought their guns around.

Just above them, on a rise, Quentin took his shot.

FORTY-TWO

When Katerina came upon Clint and Mano lying in the dirt with three other men, she thought they were all dead.

She dismounted and hurried to Mano first. Immediately, she saw that he was breathing, although he was bleeding from a wound in his side.

"Mano . . ." she said, shaking him.

Clint awoke when he heard a girl's voice. He put his hand to his head, came away with blood. He'd been shot in the head, but he didn't know how badly.

He got to his feet, survived a moment of dizziness, then saw Katerina crouching over Mano.

"Katerina," he said.

She turned and looked at him.

"What are you doing here?"

"I came to warn you," she said. "I heard Montero and Antonia talking. She was telling him to steal the bull."

"Antonia?"

"*Sí,*" she said, "I knew she did not love my father. She wants to sell the bull."

Clint looked around. The cart and team were gone, with the bull, and with their horses. His head was pounding, blood was seeping down the side of his head. He took a bandanna from his pocket and held it to his head.

"What happened here?" she asked.

"These three jumped us," he said, "but I'd swear . . ."

"What?"

He walked to all three men, checked them, and found them dead. Then he stood over Steiger and stared down at him.

"What is it?" she asked again.

"I could swear this one fired and missed," he said. "So how did I get this head wound?"

"Mano is shot," she said.

Clint hurried over to Mano and crouched on the other side of him. He examined the wound.

"It went through," he said. "It's not bad. In fact, he's coming around."

"Wha—what happened?" Mano asked. "Ow! That hurts."

"It should," Clint said. "You got shot."

"Where?"

"In the side." Clint took the bandanna from

Mano's neck, wadded it up, and put it inside his shirt, over the wound.

"Katerina?" Mano said, looking at her.

"*Sí, mi amor,*" she said, touching his face.

"You'll have to stay with him," Clint said.

"Where are you going?" Mano asked.

"I've got to track the cart," Clint said. "I have to get back that bull, not to mention my horse." He looked at Katerina. "I'll have to take your horse. I'll leave you the water, and come back."

"What if you do not come back?" she asked.

"I will."

He stood up, took the canteen from her saddle, and set it down next to her.

"You do not have to track them," she said.

"What do you mean?"

"I know where they went. I heard them talking."

"Where?"

"The mission."

"Where's the mission, and what's there?"

"I will tell you . . ."

When Clint rode up to the mission two hours later, he saw the tracks from the cart's wheels. They looked like they led right to the church.

He glanced around, didn't see anyone, but he heard a faint mixture of horses whinnying and men conversing inside the church. He dismounted, grabbed Katerina's rifle from her scabbard, then slapped the horse to send him trotting away.

He ran to the side of the adobe building, moved toward a window. When he looked inside, he saw them—Antonia, Montero, and what appeared to be a priest. And yes, the bull and the cart were inside. The church was in disrepair and he could see a hole in the wall on the other side, obviously where they had driven the cart in.

He flattened himself against the wall and closed his eyes against the momentary surge of pain. He had tied the bandanna around his head and put his hat over it. The bleeding had stopped, but he still had a headache.

There were more voices than the ones coming from the church. Someone was behind the building, laughing. He moved along the wall until he reached the back, then peered around. Four men, two of them well over six feet, three wearing guns and one—one of the big men—holding a rifle. They were standing in front of a corral, passing around a bottle of whiskey and having a grand old time. Inside the corral, still saddled, were their horses, as well as Eclipse and Mano's horse.

"That was a hell of a shot, *amigo*," one of them said to the big man with the rifle.

"I didn't kill him, though," the man said. "Montero should have let me kill him."

"I think the *señora* would not let him," another man said. "I think she was sweet on the gringo."

"Still shoulda killed him," the big man said.

Clint thought he remembered a third shot before

he blacked out. Must have been this man's rifle he'd heard.

Seven. He counted seven, four outside, three inside. Only he probably didn't have to worry about Antonia, or the priest. Only Montero. That meant killing these four took priority. Once they were handled, there was only Montero.

And only one way to do it.

Surprise.

He set the rifle down against the wall, stepped out into the open, right hand down by his gun.

"Hey, *amigos!*" he called.

The four men looked at him and stopped laughing—then they went for their guns, the whiskey bottle dropping from one man's hand.

Clint drew and fired four times, so swiftly that the last shot had struck its target before the whiskey bottle hit the ground and shattered . . .

"What was that?" Antonia said.

"Shots," Padre Pete said. "You should have killed Adams."

"It can't be him," Montero said.

"Can't it?"

Montero gave Antonia a stony look.

"You should have killed him," she said.

"You told me not to."

"I told you to get the bull, no matter what you had to do."

"And I did."

"All right," Padre Pete said. "*Señora*, you stay here while Carlos and I go out and handle Adams."

"Handle him?"

Padre Pete swept his robes back, exposing two holstered, pearl-handled colts on his hips.

"Handle," he said.

FORTY-THREE

Clint grabbed his rifle, walked to the four fallen men to make sure they were dead. They were. Quickly, he reloaded his pistol, just in time to see the two men step from the church through the hole in the wall. One was Montero, the other the priest—who was wearing two guns.

"Montero," Clint said. "Where is Antonia?"

"She is inside, *señor*," Montero said. "She will stay there until we have dealt with you."

"Dealt with me?" Clint asked. "You and the priest?"

"Padre Pete," the priest said. "You are Clint Adams?"

"I am."

"A pleasure to meet you."

"I'm not used to seeing gun-toting priests," Clint said.

"I wasn't always a priest," Pete said. "We all have pasts, Adams. Mine was . . . unsavory, until I came here and discovered . . . God."

"And kept your guns."

Pete shrugged.

"Some habits die hard."

"But you're not really an ordained priest, are you?" Clint asked.

"Well, no, not technically."

"Good," Clint said. "I've never killed a priest before, and I don't want to start now."

"That remains to be seen."

"Look, Father—"

"Padre," he said, "Padre Pete."

"Padre, I don't know what your part is in this—"

"We—you, me, Carlos here—have all fallen under Antonia's spell at one time or another. We have that in common."

"And I guess some of you are still under her spell," Clint said.

"I guess we are."

"Well," Clint said, "you and I don't have that in common. I've come for the bull."

"You have to go through us to get it," Pete said.

Clint indicated the four dead men and said, "I guess it's a little too late for me to talk you out of it."

"Oh, yes," Pete said. "Too late."

"Carlos?" Clint asked.

"Too late, *señor*," Montero said, and went for his gun.

Antonia heard the shots, folded her arms beneath her breasts, and waited, holding her breath. When Clint Adams came through the hole in the wall, she let her breath out.

"We better get going, Antonia," he said.

She nodded.

Clint was driving the cart out of Mission, with Antonia next to him, and Eclipse and Mano's horse tied to the back, when he saw the *rurales* riding in, Captain Ortiz at the head of the column.

"Oh, great," Clint muttered.

"Do not worry," she said wearily.

He looked at her, then said, "You mean . . . him, too?"

"Antonia," Captain Ortiz said, reining in. "You are looking as lovely as ever."

Clint held his breath. If Ortiz was still under Antonia's spell, she could have the man arrest him. There was no way he could fight the entire company of *rurales*.

"*Gracias, Capitán.*"

"And Mr. Adams," Ortiz said, "where are you off to now?"

"We are taking this bull to my husband, *Capitán*," Antonia said.

Ortiz looked past them, but all the bodies were hidden in the church.

"Well," he said, "do not let me stop you." He waved to his men. *"Ándale."*

The column went around them.

"You could have used them against me."

"No," she said, "I would rather go back to Don Pablo."

"We better put as much distance between us and here before they find the bodies in the church," Clint said, snapping the reins.

FORTY-FOUR

WYOMING

Clint rode onto Bill Werter's spread a month and a half after he had left. Werter came out of his house and walked around the cart, peering in.

"Wow," he said, "he's a monster."

"Yeah, he is," Clint said, dropping down from the cart.

Elizabeth came out to look as well.

"Did you have adventures?" she asked him.

"Any trouble?" Werter asked.

Clint touched his hat, which was hiding his head wound.

After he and Antonia had returned to the rancho, they sent men out to retrieve Katerina and Mano, and sent for a doctor to treat their wounds. Then he had left, and Mano had stayed, with Katerina looking after him and Don Pablo hovering over them. The *rurales* had not come to the rancho, even though they must have discovered all the bodies. Don Pablo had enough influence to scare them away.

But why tell Werter all of that? Or maybe just wait 'til later. For now he just said, "Everything went smoothly. Not a hitch."

"Really?" Elizabeth asked, looking disappointed. "No adventures?"

Werter came over and slapped Clint on the back.

"Thanks for delivering El Duque, Clint, but why don't you just make up some kind of story to satisfy her?"

Clint thought for a moment, then said, "I can probably do that."

Watch for

THE PINKERTON JOB

378th novel in the exciting GUNSMITH series

from Jove

Coming in June!

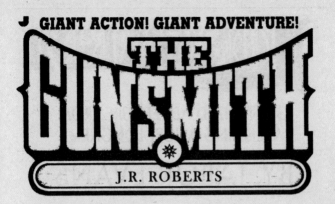

GIANT-SIZED ADVENTURE FROM AVENGING ANGEL LONGARM.

BY TABOR EVANS

penguin.com/actionwesterns